Also by Ellis Sharp

I0533885

Novels

Unbelievable Things
Walthamstow Central
Intolerable Tongues
To Wetumpka
Lamees Najim

Short Fiction

The Aleppo Button
Lenin's Trousers
(with Mac Daly) *Engels on Video*
To Wanstonia
Driving My Baby Back Home
Aria Fritta
Quin Again, and other stories
Dead Iraqis: Selected Short Stories

Non-Fiction

Sharply Critical

ELLIS SHARP

THE DUMP

Zoilus Press

First published in Great Britain by Zoilus Press, 1998

Reprinted 2019

ISBN 0952202875

THE DUMP

for Ken MacLeod

Seventeen million dead last year, not bad, not bad at all, eh? As for me, you. Be patient. Allow me a breath. The game will soon be up. A couple of hours at best. I gather my dregs. Where words are scarce... Eh? Call me a whirl-brain that talks whatever comes uppermost. Frantic-mad with evermore unrest. I gather my dregs of energy, yes. For the last struggle. Time, now, eh? To take up some of the ragged ends left behind. To clear up the facts of the matter. To illuminate the situation. Better still to eliminate it. I shall contribute a decisive step in the physics of elementary particles, something of a highly algebraic nature! Not overlooking the obscure parts in my own fortunes. A rump of words. The privy corners of my mazëd mind. Something to get your teeth into. Really? Really. I speak fondly. After that you will find me obmutescent. Meantime, though comatose and drowsy, I will tell lengthily the lousy things which occurred. Sound a sennet! Scalp glabrous, face glaciated, battered by hours and days. Fossicking around. I left home with a light heart, speaking English well, and strong in arithmetic, bah! And now? A.J.'s Annual Party? Adventures of Master F.J.? In moments of extremity every man becomes an orator. Women too, I suppose. Speke, Parrot! Talk of orts, worts, banana skins. Of time upon a once, interminable. Drink deep, ride hard. I have greasy hair and whistle every S in my vocabulary, what's it to you, mister? Miss? Mizz. Hark! I hear from the heart of the hills I suppose the thunder of the imprisoned river. Twelve hours, twelve bounteous hours are gone. At least. Eh? Here in The Dump, yes. Top o' the Heap! Ah, the cosmic abundance of helium! At least fifty miles from the nearest metaphor. So it feels. Picking your nose, you pick your way across the ash. All over. A soft drift of syntax. A colon lying on its side, staring at me. Oxidised scraps of news yellow as my stumps. The King of the Belgians is suffering from acute heart trouble and is unable to move about. Good. Delighted to hear it. Nice to hear I'm not the only one. I shall sing with the miller of the Dee. Pen, ink, and paper are cold vehicles. Stop? Commas. Black, like grit. Indispensable in such surroundings. Here and there a spiky zed. Trousers, boots, grey with dust. The occasional lustreless gerund. How deeply *unpoetical* the age and all one's surroundings are.

The level waste, the rounding gray. Streak of glimmering sunshine, say. No. Just grass and barren silent stones. I think not. A ridge topped (yes, topped) with dead tree trunks, sneezewood, say, and (naturally) stinkwood. Can't be. Verisimilitude demands... Eh? Ruins overgrown with marginalia. Light of the westering sun, then gone. The darkness. Rolling clouds speckled with débris. Fused metal and concrete. A burned-out place. This septic isle, this ordure of Windsors. Upon it you lower your arse, your gaze. Stones and wiring, overgrown with dark, sticky weeds. And the stench! Fetch me sweet marjoram! What defects, what darkness. Broken signs. Hardocks, hemlock, nettles. Singing "Polly Wolly Doodle," day after day. Fancy a game of Kick the Can? Or King of the Hill? Don't wait for me, I won't be back. Just sit quietly if you wish. A blind man's bluff. Face streaked with dirt. Eyes bloodshot and red as Joe McKenny's. Smile you my speeches, as I were a fool? Melten da! Fatel era why a keel? What's on? What's happening? Eleemosynary, my dear Wassermann, I am not. No more of that. I hope in time to make myself opaque. You heard several stories? You're about to hear the real one, mister. I should know. I was in charge of the burial detail. A tongue, tongues! Of fire. See, hear. The smoke. The golden ointment. You want to watch what you're saying. Your self, mister, eh? Watch. Or miss. Miss everything. Watch. Tick-tock. Up there. Scrap of blue sky, then gone. Over there. Churned-up mud, as far as the eye can squint. The snapped, burned trees. Ground full of blocks and blocking steel. Everything getting dark, brittle. Century's end, probably. Can't be sure. Perhaps the year 4462853 S.E.C. Perhaps the twenty-first, who knows? Don't try telling me this is latter Lammas, matey. What a period. A clue, quick! How's the wind? Thrrraaaarrrp! Interminable, the long evening-ends, flatulence, storm and thunder, flashes of bright light, no getting away from it. You want to watch your tongue! Eh? How live I then, which thus draw forth my days? I sing as the boy does by the burying ground. This day then, let us not... Encolpius speaking. Call me Berserk, I like it. Call me Egbert Souse! Wash Jones, perhaps. Though somewhat battered I look nothing at all like the puffy, shifty *Rektorat* of the University of

Freiburg in 1933-34. In another time, another place, perhaps I shall be Charles Le Boeuf, Comte d'Osmoy. Quaxo. Major Jack Hobbs. The Marquis de Lafayette, Postmaster General (retired). Or Everett Ruess. Eh? Alexander Supertramp? No! Call me Bronterre. I am very heavy. Call me Schüler, yes. Bernard Schüler! Come and enjoy all the fun of the Zirkus Schüler! My grotesque girls will do their very best! Please ignore all the stories! The people! Changing and changing. Alice! The young girl Judith, the wife Clarisse! The trap. Eh? Call me Switchman. O, how that name befits my composition! What's that? More good news! Cholera in the Sudan has killed at least 700 people! The old diseases are making a come-back, hallelujah! The death toll but the toxic tit of the iceberg as many areas in south Sudan are inaccessible due to the civil war. Said the Belgian branch of Médecins Sans Frontières. Reuter – Nairobi. More good news! Syria is building a poison gas factory in the northern city of Aleppo. It's said. So time. Time to – Split? Obscurely here alone. Ill, with swellings. Snowed in. Larynx frozen and just a hint of cerebral edema. Wind, throbbings. Inflammation. Pemphigus, possibly. Definite symptoms of pellagra! Décrépit, poudreux, sale, abject, visqueux, fêlé. Play me the Cancer Symphony! Dorsal trouble in the blood, that too. The. Long. Disease. Is. Yes. The. Worst. Devise betimes some drams! Bronterre? After Bronterre O'Brien, you oaf! My father wanted a complete subversion of the existing order! Can hear, just about, Willie Nelson singing "Sentimental Journey". Can hear, just about, J. J. Cale singing "Days Go By". What's more I have a bad cold. Also (*entre nous*) a little feverish. My teeth, my discoloured stumps, long since gone. But still toothache! The fact is. Is. The TV cunts. They have theirs but no bite, no bite at all. They all look so fucking HAPPY. Shit, must watch my language! I, miserable impotent, moi, celibate and slack and tight as a whiskery retentive nonagenarian nun, I think there is something wrong with my liver. Twenty ailments, at least. Fetch me the latest *Diagnostic and Statistical Manual of Mental Disorders*! I deny absolutely the stories about coma, amnesia, furor, automatism, chronic hallucinations and dementia! All lies, from beginning to end! I know nothing about an eight-day travelling clock and a generous Dutchman! I have never been to Mexico! Pifflocation? Piffle! Famish an aged beggar at your gates, you bastards. World starvation? What's that – 850 million people in the world are severely malnourished? Time for another United Nations World Food Summit with first- class air travel and luxury hotels, essential for any civilised discussion of these mattters! There is a prosperity that a man findeth in misfortunes, eh? You will know of course what happened to poor Jenny after she left for Paris on Wednesday 17 December, 1862. Thankfully, sometimes, a few distractions. To take your mind off it all. Seventeen million dead last year, not bad, not bad at all. And that was just the preventable infectious diseases! Details, did you say? Certainly. Only too happy to. 3.1 million from TB, 4.4 million from respiratory diseases like pneumonia, 3.1 million from typhoid and dysentery, 2.1 million from malaria. Over one million from measles! And in the UK alone 576 deaths in police custody between 1985 and 1995. 24,000 civilians killed or maimed by landmines every year, with the full backing – cheers! – of Her Majesty's Government. Hawk aircraft and British Alvis armoured vehicles sold – rah, rah, rah! – to Indonesian killers. Keeping the numbers down. Everyone – British Aerospace, Vosper Thorneycroft, Vickers Defence Systems – doing their bloody bit. Washed down with an invigorating squirt courtesy of Tactica water cannon. And Mahmoud Jamayyal dead. And Latin American police putting guns in children's mouths – guns made in Birmingham, U.K. I'm proud to say. And pleased as Punch to announce that when Anthony Ginting, a bus conductor from North Sumatra, was beaten by the police, they stabbed his head with a screwdriver manufactured in Scruton and smashed his fingers with a hammer from Hammersmith. Damchoe Pemo, pregnant Tibetan, repeatedly beaten with a baton from Britain! Electric shocks? Blowtorches? Shackles? Drills? Come to Esher for all the fun of the fair! Mais je divague. Bored already, I bet. Who wants to read stuff like this when you could be comfy and warm and faraway, eh? But thanks anyway for the diversions. A bit of excitement never did anyone any harm. The distant piercing thump a powerful bomb exploding. The satisfying collapse of apparently solid, sturdy structures. The delightfully abrupt disappearance of old friends. Broken windows in Marx and Spengler's. Wreckage. The donkey bray of sirens. Anything to get away from all this. Come on! A soap. A nice liceless ice. A good yarn. Thomas the Blue Conformist Tank Engine. Take up your Pipes and puff away. He was by all accounts a sinister person. Full of resentment and frustration. Everything at sixes and sevens. Put various twos and twos together, get the whole story bent. A spicy literary biography, perhaps. A bit on the side. Original and curious positions. I used to wonder what the trick would be at fifty – aleatoricism? A fizzing this, a sparkling that. A G and T. An ABC narrative. The anecdotes of Hugh Severance. An afternoon of vigorous intercourse. Three long raw days of bitter invective concerning the relative merits of Bodley MS 851 and Bodley MS 581. On the fourth day jokes. Jokes about humorous or unusual incidents. Tristana's amputation. Lusty Robin and his dog. Little Pete and his tiny organ. Thynne, Pynche, Lem, Ledger, Hitchprick, Hal, Spinks, Dribble, Hecuba, Fricker and Jigger and Jug. Winnebago with his black flowery orbits so reminiscent of a transexual's. Zelma Van Riper! Petulant Darkbloom, with Clinton Dangerfield. Mr Kite. Mr Japp. Ms. Kapp. Zeeta. Mure. Death's refuse. Baron von Tink. Gerry and Jerry. Jerry and Tom. Scented Tom and malodorous Viv. Ron and Em (the filthy pair would collogue for hours). Ron and Effie. Dick and Fanny. Not forgetting, no. Bill and Will. Willie and Wally. Al and Ally. Miss N. Flood. Nature's dregs. Tiny O'Toole. Jones. Sebastian Melmoth, is he here too? And bugger me if it isn't Oscar! In this bottomless hell. And Giacinta, my gitanilla? Never! Chin up old man, stiff upper, cock too one of these days I wouldn't be at all surprised. Fingers crossed, fist clenched, oh Jesus! "Come up, Captain Harris." He gripped Wiley Post by the throat. His face went purple, he began to make odd choking noises. You and I begin and end here, eh? We go back a long way, eh, my old ape, my slithery amphibian. And now back for one last fight. Old worm; old miserable weed. Slime dreaming of slime in a climate of hydrated iron oxide. The expendables. The glory guys. On a tequila high, thinking that life's not so bad after all, eh? The possibility – the dream – of breaching The Great Barrier. I will set out for Ireland tomorrow se'nnight. Tomorrow at ten I shall take a train. Tomorrow, comrades... Next week, sisters... The day it rained, for example. At first it seemed like an invigorating start to an otherwise dull day. The time I estimate to have been around ten a.m. and the dim sun was just beginning its slow, washed-out crawl over Hackney. The ecru wastes. Many natives of The Dump were still not up. Most, probably. Out of sight, dozing and comfy. Or wailing softly. Gnashing their stumps. Or awake but still huddled in drifts of old warm newspaper. Awake yet inert. Like Dorothy and William Wordsworth we sat shivering for three-quarters of an hour. Titillating themselves with logodaedaly, possibly. At best sucking on yesterday's core, I imagine. Others, Early Risers like myself, were already up and about. Up and about, can you believe! Such naïvety. How we deserved that piercing upper case. How the Old Timers chuckled at the antics of the Early Risers! How Tristan L'Hermite and Orrery and Huff and Dr Presto wheezed and Madox and Molkin and Boris de Schloezer giggled! How peeping Parvisol toothlessly grinned! How Vanhomrigh and Ogle screeched. How Beaumont hooted! Such droll efforts at hygiene and good grooming! Peripeteia and piss! Hope lighting a feeble lamp! Poor damnéd souls still going through the old, old motions. As if still in salaried employment, say. Biological clock throbbing in tune to capitalism's awesome requirements. Six dot dot one five already, gosh! Emerge from warmth, into the cold, bladder bursting. Up and about in the night's embers, groggy with fatigue. Down the corridor, piss, the old motions. Then downstairs. Gliding along a ghost hallway to a spectral kitchen in order to switch on a dematerialised kettle. Refreshed by gulps of scalding imaginary Lapsang Souchong. Upstairs again. Moving in slow motion towards the grey eye of the little shaving mirror. Smiling one's best *autoritätsgläubig* smile. Reaching for the aerosol spray, getting ready to press it, the foam spewing out into the palm of your hand. Mustn't be late for work! The gulped bowl of cereal, the wolfed toast, the race to the office, the hands of clocks and timepieces speeding towards eight-thirty, nine, nine-fifteen. Up and about, stretching, yawning, unloosing a sequence of quick, brief, spurting farts redolent of creamed mushrooms and succulent beef stew. Brushing one's yellow, rotting teeth. Igniting, for those with the wherewithal, a camp fire. Attempting toast while dreaming, say, of crispy sea snails with parmesan and tomato confit. Gnawing an old stale bun whilst recalling the good old days. Talk about Proust's biscotte (first draft, you bastards)! Foie gras with fig purée! Chickpea blinis with crab! Tour d'Argent duck cooked in blood with a side dish of crunchy sugared lamb. That glorious little bistro down the side street by the abattoir where we feasted on salmon in basil and garlic followed by lamb with grapefruit zest while three streets away the riot police had a laugh battering the students and the blacks! Ah, the lobster medallions with 17,000 Bq/kg of invigorating technetium-99! The marinated veal slices with saute of asparagus Parotid! Our submaxillary and sublingual glands gushed like ruptured pipes in the domain of a newly-privatised water company neglecting capital expenditure on maintenance in favour of an even bigger dividend for its anal retentive 4-wheel-drive Surrey shareholders. Gone, quite gone. Half-lewdly sucking on a prized carrot, attempting to extinguish the dream of a D-section tin of pâté de foie gras, a fillet of sea bream with morille mushrooms. Out! Get thee gone! Slobbering and sobbing and weeping and dribbling and feasting like a rabid frothing dog on a foul strip of raw and reeking bacon. Another ordinary Dump day. And then, I estimate at about ten, it happened. That lukewarm spray. That pitter-patter of first drops. Pitter-patter upon the hatches, the planks, the cloth hoods of The Early Risers, the corrugated iron sheets. "Rain!" cried Bodfish excitedly. Glorious, glorious rain! He ran for his mug to catch some. I stared deliriously at the sky. In no time at all my hair and collar were soaked. The Old Timers remained inert, out of sight, sceptical, in the grip of diasparactivity. Incontinent, often. No need here to heed wheedling bourgeois calls for restraint or bottles! Here the perfect place for piss-a-beds! Dribbling a quiet peaceful not unpleasurable dribble. Warming one's thighs with yellowish-green tributaries very reminiscent of the Borve River south of the A857. Capital spent. Not so The Early Risers. Full of vim and pep, sickeningly eager. We abandoned our fires, our rudimentary breakfasts. We gave up our studies, put away our Plato, our copiously annotated copies of *Middlemarch*, efforts at a diatessaron. Those in holes and ditches scrambled excitedly out of their holes and ditches. Those under planks and iron sheets sipping the last of their watery tea pushed aside planks and iron sheets. Such animation! How those of us wearing anoraks jerked back our hoods and began to run. To and fro, hither and thither, sideling. Arms outstretched, can you believe! Some breaking into spontaneous applause, like old style communists. Some excitedly breaking wind. Some whispering the Lord's Prayer. Some tripping and crashing to the ground but up in no time, no time at all! Spitting out broken teeth, licking off the dribbles of blood, pushing back protruding splinters of bone, how they laughed and shrieked. "Glorious, glorious rain!" repeated Bodfish, holding out his tin mug. His four eyes blinked repeatedly with nervous excitement. A lump of shadow the size of a double-decker bus raced across the surface of The Dump and vanished into the nearest fumes. I put it down to optical trickery stemming from my already waning eyesight or vitamin deficiency. The back of my hand was yellowish and glistening. I tongued it, grimaced. "What is it?" said Bodfish. "What's the matter?" A question of gross stupidity. "The Dump is the matter," I might have retorted. But did not. "Tastes funny," I replied. "Sort of bitter." "You can bet your boots it's acid rain," put in Hoadly. "All the pollution. Car exhausts. Factories. You bet that's what it is." Hoadly was a beefy, red-faced man of about fifty. A former chef. His knowledge of air pollutants was extensive. Bodfish was also a beefy, red-faced man of about fifty but of course could not be confused with Hoadly because of his extra two eyes. Leo, by contrast, was only twenty-six, skinny and pale. Leo was the only one among us who had realised the significance of the fleeting shadow. He scanned the sky, raised his telescope. "An aerostat!" he cried. "See! Right above us!" Everyone in the vicinity looked up, catching the full force of the second shower. This was of a greenish hue. Bodfish threw down his mug angrily. "This is disgusting," he said. "Whatever can it be?" "Work it out for yourself," snickered Leo. "I

14

don't get it," spat Bodfish. "I feel sure it must have been approved by the Food Advisory Committee, an impartial government body made up of representatives of Marks & Spencer, Unilever, Dalgety, Northern Foods, International Foods, Tesco, J. Sainsbury, Cadbury Schweppes, Reckitt & Colman, Scottish & Newcastle, Carlsberg-Tetley, Whitbread, the Scottish Salmon Growers, Marine Harvest, St Ivel, United Biscuits, Glaxo, SmithKline Beecham, Smith & Newphew, and Boots the chemist." His eyes flickered uneasily. Leo laughed sardonically. "It's the people in that aerostat up there," he said. "They're pissing on us." Leo wiped the dew from the lens of his telescope and scanned the aerial device anew. "And if I'm not very much mistaken it's the Queen who is pissing on us now. Here, take a look." He passed me the telescope. Beneath the huge royal blue flanks of the balloon hung, dead centre, a cylinder. From the cylinder roared a pillar of controlled fire. Beneath this, on wires, swung a cage. The cage, which had a white chest-high wall running round it, contained around a dozen figures. What with my weak arms, the excitement, and the surprising speed of the balloon, it was difficult to focus. What might have been a General jerked sideways and turned into a pair of Princes and a senior police officer. These three figures at once abruptly metamorphosed into a pair of sallow, scrawny buttocks. I realised that there was some sort of sliding panel in the wall of the cage. Someone – a woman – was crouching on the floor of the cage with her skirt hitched up around her waist. I glimpsed a wisp of pubic hair, the brown dot of an anus. The buttocks seemed to deflate, the thigh muscles to tighten. Next bright amber jets of urine pumped out through the open panel and fell, twisting and spreading across a brief, rare shaft of sunlight. Our souls swam in blessed waters of ease. And then the woman stood up and stared down at us. I recognised her sour, wrinkled face at once. "Leo's right," I said, trembling. "It's her. Elizabeth Vagina! The cunt!" As I was speaking a fresh shower hit me, fouling my words. "It's a lie!" screamed Bodfish. "A dirty filthy lie!" He snatched the telescope, focused, thrust it back at me. "Nothing like!" he said triumphantly. Adding: "See this." Bodfish produced from his pocket his treasure. A brand-new silver tenpenny piece. He pointed a finger at the Queen's silhouette. "See? That radiance! That beauty! Looks nothing like that old hag up there!" Leo turned to me. "How long has he been in The Dump?" he enquired, weakly. "Years," I replied. "Years and years and years." "But doesn't he read the papers?" "Evidently not." "Queen of YUK," said Leo. "Short for Ye U.K." Eh? What's this nonsense? What is this Dump? You cannot seriously expect the reader to believe that the royal family are in the habit of ascending in aerostats for the sole purpose of relieving their bodily wastes upon their subjects! Whoever heard of such a thing? "Now you watch it my lad," said Bodfish, addressing Leo. "I've had enough of your nonsense." He raised his right fist. "Don't mock." He was about to say something else when the potato hit him smack on the crown of his head. "Shit!" he kelmaned. "That hurt! That fucking fucking hurt! Whatever the fuck it was." He glared kelmanly at Leo, holding him responsible. Tears brimming in all four bloodshot angry eyes. "A potato, I believe," I contributed. "Doubtless hurled by one of those hot-air hooligans." Bodfish snatched the telescope back, angled it. Focused. "Bastard!" he screamed. "The dirty, dirty bastard! The fucking, dirty, dirty, fucking bastard!" "What ails you, Bodfish?" I whispered, my voice muted by a passing drift of smoke. The former trades-union official was on his knees, scrabbling around, clawing at the loose scattering of detritus. "Got you!" Bodfish held up the potato. "Potato!" he said scornfully. He held it out. I caught a whiff, flinched. "Potato," he repeated in a low angry whisper. Its slime fouled his palms. Bitterly he hurled it hard as he could. It soared away, vanishing amid the smoke from a pile of burning tyres. "It was the Duke," he said, sorrowfully, wiping his hands on a Westminster Abbey teatowel. "The Duke himself. I recognised him from photographs. I recognised the uniform. The Grand Order of the People's Republic of Romania. The rancid scowl. The hatchet-faced bag of scum," he added colourfully. "You mean–?" I gasped. He nodded. He seemed to have aged ten years in as many minutes. Twenty. Thirty. He shook his head. "The Duke himself," he muttered. "Coming here of all places. To laugh at us. To piss on us. To shit all over us. Fucking foreigner. Greasy Greek. I never liked him, never." Bodfish was visibly crumbling (not to mention the invisibles clawing his innards). His dark, oily hair was white, as if someone had emptied a bag of flour over him. The flour had coated his face, drained his cheeks. Cracks were spreading across his brow, around his eyes. Bodfish clenched his fists. "And after all I've done for that family! The flags I've waved on Empire Day! The parades, the processions! The weddings and funerals! Not overlooking three o'clock on Christmas Day. Not missed it once in over forty years!" Sobbing, he fingered the lump on his head. By now the aerostat was a blue blob over Highgate, sailing fast back to the great green palace lawn in WC1. Bodfish shook his fist at the blob. I took back the telescope, peered. Yes, they were all there. The florid, elephantine heir, H.R.H. Prince Charles Philip Arthur George Windsor, Prince of Wales, Earl of Chester, Duke of Cornwall, Duke of Rothesay, Earl of Carrick, Baron of Renfrew, Lord of the Isles and Prince and Great Steward of Scotland. The rancid lecherous foul-mouthed Duke. Coarse, beefy, addled, blustering Andy. Inane Edward. Sozzled Margaret. "The dirty scum!" howled Bodfish. He began punching the ground and at once cut himself on an empty can of tomatoes. Punch! Punch! Punch! Soon his hands were two sodden, bloody shreds, strands of Italian tomato mingled with torn flesh. Pain didn't seem to bother him any more. He sat there for the rest of the morning and all afternoon. In the afternoon it really did rain, a cold perpetual pelting rain that continued until nightfall by which time Bodfish quietened down. He gave up beating the ground and lay down, his head propped on a solidified bag of cement. He must have cut a vein he shouldn't have because in the morning he'd become a stiff Z in a dark puddle of blood. Leo and I watched the rats, dogs and starlings taking turns to tuck in. "He learned," said Leo. "A bit late in the day, but he learned." "What a consolation," I said sarcastically. "No, no." Leo shook his head. "Perception's the thing. All it needs is for everyone to learn what Bodfish learned." "Fat chance," said I. "You wait and see. Revolutions happen when you least expect them. Remember Lenin in Switzerland. Old and tired before his time. Given up all hopes. *We, the old ones, may never live to see the decisive battles of the coming revolution.*

Next thing – hey presto! 27 February 1917. Shooting has started. The crowds on Gospitalnaia, Paradnaia, and other streets are very large. Life's full of surprises, eh?" "Let us give poor Bodfish a Christian burial," I said, ignoring his nonsense. "You must be fucking crackers," Leo replied coldly. "For the sake of his poor wife and children." "I'm not arguing. I'm off. Coming?" Wiping the sleep from my eyes I observed that Leo had his sleeping bag and his rucksack of paperbacks with him. He meant business. "Oh very well," I said irritably. I knew that I could not afford to be parted from Leo just yet. "Which way are we going?" "East," said Leo. "I always feel more comfortable in the East End." I hurried after him. Nearby a huddle of wretches were grouped excitedly around a flickering TV set. The sight is not so rare as you might imagine. Technicians and electricians come hurtling into The Dump at regular intervals, propelled there by redundancy or dicky hearts or bad marriages. Fiddling with wrecked TVs seems to keep them happy, the screwdriver in their hand, a gleam of interest in their eyes. They find batteries, wires, rig up aerials, get TVs to work. They talk excitedly of radiowaves and transmitters. Some think of radioing for help but of course it's been tried, doesn't work. There is a field of electrical disturbance. Or perhaps jamming. Very mysterious. All possible ways of communicating with The Real World are closed. This has encouraged a sect which subscribes to the theory that everyone in The Dump is dead. You sometimes see them lying apathetically in large cardboard boxes bearing the names of supermarket chains, refusing all offers of food. "We are all dead," they whisper, and soon they are. Not this lot. They were watching the news. On the screen a tower block belched smoke. Police with batons drummed with animation the shoulders and raised arms of young men and women. Silver churns were tipped and an arc of milk met the lip of a drain. A man wearing a jacket and tie mouthed silent words. We hurried on until the TV fell from view behind mounds of putrefying cabbages. "Ah well," I said, fingering my damp clothes and smoothing my sodden hair. "It's not every day you are pissed on by the Queen." "Oh yes it is," said Leo. To my surprise – I really wasn't expecting it to happen again quite so suddenly – there came the cry, "AEROSTAT!" Worse: the plural. "Quick," said Leo, grimacing. He sank into the nearest trench and began hurriedly covering himself in sheets of crisp unblemished corrugated cardboard. Leo handed me the telescope. "Feel free to watch if you want," he said. Then he vanished from sight. Surely he was wrong, I thought. This is nothing more than a simple balloon race! A colourful and graceful sight. Balloon after balloon, brightly coloured, many bearing the names of their sponsors (fizzy drink, car manufacturer, airline, mobile phone). I counted fifty, eighty, more and more, stately, gently drifting towards us, blown by the current, heading east, north, north-north-east, from Westminster and Highgate, like galleons of old. Despite my situation and my toothache and the inclement weather I felt a glow of pride to be British. I swung the telescope with trembling hand. They were getting nearer, I could hear the faint hiss of the roaring flames that kept them aloft, could see the tiny figures in the baskets. I focused the telescope. More than a mere race, I realised. Evidently some sort of state occasion. In one balloon I could see the Archbishop of Canterbury, various archdeacons, deacons, prelates. Plump shiny bespectacled faces, crisp white dog collars, red robes, a golden mitre. An adjacent brown balloon contained several members of the cabinet. Scanning the blue balloon I excitedly spotted three famous newsreaders and a famous weather forecaster. What else? A green balloon containing the managing directors of privatised utilities. A purple balloon containing sports personalities. A black balloon containing comedians. An ultramarine balloon containing pop singers. Others containing snooker players, darts champions, cricketers. Not forgetting merchant bankers and city brokers. Landowners. Those in line for the throne in the event of a distressing sequence of assassinations and cataclysmic events, including the eldest sons of Dukes of Royal Blood, Marquesses, the Bishops of London, Durham and Winchester, Barons and Knights Grand Cross of the Bath. Last of all came the Masters in Lunacy, silvery-haired and flushed, looking like elderly distinguished parliamentarians. Floating all across that clear blue sky. I glanced across at Leo's ditch. The cardboard did not stir. Asleep, perhaps. Not knowing what he was missing. Ah, the grandeur of the occasion! I could hear the blast of trumpets, royal heralds. Any moment now the Red Arrows would whizz past trailing scarlet smoke. Any moment a pair of Spitfires would pass overhead, wings dipping in salute. There were less people watching than I expected. I counted about thirty, all new arrivals, all staring enraptured like myself. I was still staring through the telescope, trying to focus on an acclaimed female columnist, when I was hit. I staggered back, stunned by the stinging shock of rain. Then smelt the familiar raw stench. Not twice in two days! Fool! Putting the telescope to my eye I scanned the baskets. I had little doubt that a couple of boozy delinquents, city brokers, were responsible. I could just imagine their silver bucket, the bottles of champagne, the popping corks. Their idea of a joke. Fool again! I couldn't believe it, I couldn't really. Panels had slid open in every basket of every balloon, exposing white buttocks, pink buttocks, brown buttocks, fat buttocks, skinny buttocks, medium buttocks, spotty buttocks, hairy buttocks, flawlessly clear buttocks, arses of every conceivable description. Together with unzipped flies, lowered shorts, raised skirts, pricks of every description, ditto cunts and pissholes and arseholes and each pissing or shitting lustily, more or less simultaneously. The first whiplash streak of piss was no sooner past then I was caught in the jet of a second which smacked into my chest and exploded across my ribs. "Run!" I heard somebody shriek. The other spectators were frantically rushing for cover, trying to burrow into mounds of rotting vegetables, throwing themselves into ditches, scrabbling desperately for something to cover themselves with. Too late, too late. There was not one that afternoon escaped scot free. The torrent was like a sudden summer thunderstorm, smashing down, making everyone sodden. But there were hailstones, too, of sorts, the size of gobstoppers, as long as sausages, brown and warm and wet, splattering everyone, coating them in gravy, in melted chocolate, in bubbling pungent onion soup. Wiping a smear of shit from my lips I kneeled by Leo's ditch, banged on his protective cardboard sheets. "Let me in!" I cried. "No," he replied. "Please!" "It won't kill you," he replied, cruelly. "But I'm going to be sick!" "All the more reason not to let you in." "But you're a socialist! You care for people! Let me in!" "Correction," said Leo coldly. "I'm a revolutionary socialist. Not a fucking philanthropist. Not a bleeding-heart liberal." "Please!" "No. Learn your lesson the hard way. It will do you good." Oh the bastard! I leaned forwards and vomited. As the vomit erupted from my throat in great scalding rhythms I could feel new slashes of rain cutting into my back, and the soft splattering of objects thudding into things from a great height. Then, suddenly, the storm was over. I could hear someone whistling a medley from *The Sound of Music*. Plus some apt Handel. I looked around. An area approximately half a mile in diameter had been transformed into a glistening swamp dappled with tiny molehills. It stank. Like myself the other newcomers were being sick, or trying, uselessly, to clean themselves. But at best all anyone could hope to do was scrape off a fraction of the filth. Then the hatch opened and Leo peeked out. He was in a maddeningly chirpy mood. He gave me a cheery wave, which I responded to with a brief, obscene gesture. This he took in his stride. "You know what this is, don't you," jeered Leo, no mark required for a rhetorical Q. "This is the famous, legendary, trickle-down effect. This is the wealth at the top of society trickling down, splitter-splatter." He wheezed at his own wit. "How does it feel, old fruit," he continued, "to be shat on by the British ruling class? If you'll forgive a stale slogan," he said sarcastically. Adding, just to rub it in: "To use a Marxist cliché. To use a dinosaur phrase of no relevance to modern life." I waved my fist, threateningly. "I'll– I'll–". But then I was sick again. Ah, The Dump, The Dump. Full of surprises. One morning you awake and find yourself lying on a dirty mattress, amid waste, desolation and smouldering rubbish. Waste as far as the eye can see. Drifts of pungent smoke. Ah, circumstances! A bit of a shock, eh? Weighing like a nightmare, eh? You remember the night before. You weren't drunk. None of your friends or relatives showed any inclinations towards arson. There was little likelihood of any of the world's top-notch terrorists targeting your particular neighbourhood. So it's a complete mystery what's happened. A gas explosion, obviously. An airliner must have crashed. And various other straws. You wait for the air ambulance, the helmeted firefighters with oxygen cylinders strapped to their backs. You search, poor fool, for a way out. That's how you came to be here. Lost and alone. One more occupant of The Dump. Condemned to an active and restless inertia amidst instability and putrefaction. The what? Its ambience? Easy-peasy. Brown as Mozart's ultimate vomit, the mire between the hillocks. Ash-grey, the plain, all around, of waste. Sour the stench of smoke and putrefaction. A smoky atmosphere, yielding royal surprises... One morning... No go. Land of abandonment and rain. Place of bottles and cast-offs. Land of things that don't work anymore. Place of the rejected, the worthless. Unwanted pages, unwanted words. Place of desolation. Talk about behind the latrines at Drancy! It's no go, here. None at all. A void, to be avoided. Here among the breakage and the waste. All that's used up, finished with, gone. One morning – give the lying bastard a name, eh? – Robinson woke up and found himself lying on a wet, dirty mattress, in the midst of an enormous region of waste, desolation and burning rubbish. Return as a dog. Second helpings. Go on! Get it over with. Here? In GB? A ludicrous idea, eh? A bit of a shock all the same, Robinson had to admit. Finding yourself in that place, of all places. The Dump. Lost there. Lost for words. Lost amid malfunctioning implements and other cast-offs. IMPRIMIS. Sodden lilac tissues, smeared pink tissues, stale bread. Bottles. Many foul-smelling cartons. Milk that's gone off. Chipped mugs. Shattered bone china. Broken glass. A cluster of stinking goosefoot, concealing a stiff rabbit. Fractured and torn deckchairs. Dead transistor radios. Stained, bloated books. Gleaming unsold remainders. Words not worth the paper they're printed on. Unending land of abandonment and rain. A disembowelled clock in a two-fifty rigor mortis. Old tyres. A solitary white fridge in a waste of mud, like... Like a last tooth in a foul mouth. Place of splayed flex, mouldy turnips. Predictable rust. Car batteries leaking acid. Insignificant puddles laced with oil and rainbow swirls. Cabbages. On the underside of the leaves a grey putrescence. Wooden crates! Plastic crates. Ten thousand thrown-out things. Many curious items, some useful, some not. Much depending on one's training, one's skills. Good eyesight.

The ability to spot iron and irons and irony. Ball valves, bits of heaters. Taps, cylinders, tanks. Vokera, Potterton, Vaillant. Ideal Standard. New potatoes! Cardboard boxes, old newspapers, magazines. Used condoms. Unused condoms past their sell-by date. Handbags and shiny raincoats fashioned out of heavily chlorinated plastic (great fun to burn). Tares. Toothbrushes with brown bristles. Bristles with dry green weed at the base. A rag, rags. Rags, old cans. Sponges. Lidless kettles. Used up, consumed, worn out, chucked out, uneaten, gone off, you name it. Bound to be there somewhere. Cartons containing unfinished takeaways. Cold rice in a tasty amber slime. Cold chips basted in vinegar, black fishskin in icy batter. Land of maggots and worms and mulches. Maggots, pretty maggots. Scoop out a quarter of a pint from my dripping injury! Don't talk to me of Inkermann. Of abandonment and rain. And the people! People? Don't pretend, you bastard. You hadn't the foggiest? Balls! You knew about the rickety population, didn't you? Yes you did, all the time. The scavengers. Befouled, unkempt, frowzy. Suffering from scurvy, malnutrition, indigestion, jail fever, lassitude. Not to mention accidents, poisonings, telangiectasis, haemorrhages. The regular loss of teeth (diseased gums, punch-ups). Ghostly figures on the horizon, almost (but not quite) out of sight, almost (but not quite) out of mind. Dump. Slump. Rump. Rump? The Queen's arse! Skirt up, knickers down, pissing on yours truly. The old hag. Felt it, saw it. Her smirk. What! Where? Surely not! I can't believe what you're saying. Hold off! Unhand me, grey-beard loon! Shan't. Not yet. Where? The Dump, that's where. Fifty square miles of garbage. A tip, literally. Heaps of piled rubbish. Rotting vegetable waste. Here and there a rusting chassis, an abandoned tyre, a dirty jam jar glinting in the sunlight. Thistles and grass, smouldering sacks, ash, thousands of empty cans. Fifty square miles? A hundred! A thousand! A hundred thousand! Big as Latin America! Nobody knows. Perhaps it is Latin America! Land of the Rumba, the Paso Doble. Of Ché and the Cha Cha Cha! Perhaps the environs of Fort Dimanche. The military dump. Exquisite pickings. Helmets. Phalluses without their ammo. Perhaps Smokey Mountain in the Philippines. The quality of the light, the quiet simplicity of the scavengers, oddly reminiscent of Vermeer. No. Wrong place. Wrong language. This is England I tell you! Can't be. What? Deaf are you? Bloody Christ! Slump-rump-dump. Slump? In confidence. In one's fortunes. In one's fiscal probity. Can this be so? The famous feelgood factor fucked-up? Feelbad, in fact? Flaming hell! Flip me! Fantastic. Leading to slumping around all day on a broken-backed sofa or a damp mattress. Oblivious to everything except the sky. A great apathy. Split, splitting into sections, my life, yes. Sectioned, so to speak. Enduring odds and ends. Making ends meet. In fits and starts. Amid shits and farts. Trying. A quiet desperation. Eyes swelling, sometimes with effort, mostly with red-hot constipation. The perturbations of flatulence. Clutching lengths of dirty string, a new way of making ends meet. I have been living like this for a long time now. Trying hard to look on the dull side of. Life? Loaf? A louse-ridden loafer. Eh? Examining an old smeared colour chart, considering which soft sheen emulsion to choose for the lounge. Considering the purchase of a Gainsborough Style 300 Electric Shower, just the thing after a matutinal jog. Wondering whether to get the natural, the buff or the red smooth paving slabs for the new patio. Not forgetting to jot down on one's list the ferrous sulphate weedkiller, the pot of Tudor Oak Garden Timbercare and the can of patio cleaner containing Benzalkonium Chloride. Ah, to relax in a deckchair on a new patio writing an appreciation of the citational imperative! Or perhaps of retroactive world-making and world-unmaking. Or perhaps a simple, racy, money-spinning synopsis of *Wuthering Heights* suitable for indolent teenagers. Mr Lockwood arrives in Yorkshire, a county in the north of England, where he meets Heathcliff, who ran away with Isabella Linton, Edgar's sister, who, Edgar, married Catherine, Hindley's sister, who dies, leaving behind a daughter, the young Cathy, who is repelled by Hareton Earnshaw, whose father is old Mr Earnshaw's son Hindley, and who is taunted by Linton, son of Isabella, who, Linton, marries Cathy, who goes back to Wuthering Heights, home of rude Joseph, where Heathcliff, who dies, tells the housekeeper, Nelly Dean, how he was dead keen on Catherine, who married the dead Edgar, which mortified him, Heathcliff, no end. *Useful questions:* 1. Describe the major wind currents in an active cumulonimbus and show the importance of the evaporation of cloud droplets to the total effect of the book. 2. Using TWO scenes in the novel in which information is communicated to characters via trails of pink lights show how important the entity VALIS [Vast Active Living Intelligence System] is in enabling Heathcliff to become master of Wuthering Heights. 3. "Property ownership: this was far more significant in the past than it is today and helped Heathcliff get his revenge." With reference to *The Sunday Times Book of the Rich* and *The German Ideology* discuss the role of bourgeois literary criticism and the National Curriculum within contemporary capitalist Britain. No. It's been done already. Okay, then. How's about a zippy musical interpretation? Dour Joseph used to play Shostakovich's Tenth at full blast, maddening Nelly, who was fond of C & W and especially Dolly Parton, unlike Mr Lockwood who was more of a Dire Straits man, whereas Heathcliff veered wildly between Led Zeppelin and Leonard Cohen, enchanting Catherine, who adored Prince, much to the anger of Edgar, a fan of Elgar, unlike Isabella, who owned every record Kate Bush had ever made, to the despair of her son, who used to shut himself away with the Cowboy Junkies, for which he was much mocked by Hareton, who greatly admired The Sex Pistols. The weather, yes. Important when you're slumping around all day on a broken-backed sofa or a damp mattress. Oblivious to everything except the sky. Dis-eased by a great apathy. The weather? Awful. Smudges of dirty cirrhus crawling across the firmament's great grey basin. Or. Or like something half-scalded, puffed-up, trapped in a bath. A tip where people live. If you can call them people. Don't say you didn't notice, didn't know. Their clothes spattered and smeared, their shoes in a dreadful state. Wildeyed. The expression all too often sly or hungry. Or dazed. Or dulled, all human interest gone, entirely gone. All our righteousnesses as filthy rags. A population divided between the newcomers, who are given to curiosity and exploration, and the old-timers, who are devoted to survival. Confusion seems inevitable. A number of newcomers arrive carrying guns and promptly go on a spree, to the perplexity of other newcomers. Sometimes you see entire families smiling at the start of the historic pageant. A crackling like fireworks, the crash of shots. One or two newcomers come tearing across the mounds of ash, bloodied and screaming. Applause. Wonderful special effects, so lifelike! Others roaring with goodnatured laughter at the plump smeared clowns falling about and slithering around in the muck. A hoot. Others dawdling, puzzled, not quite understanding what is going on. Chukka-chukka-chukka. Hey, is that the sound of semi-automatic gunfire? Is this part of the show? There's no biz– And then the realisation strikes. Everyone is running for their lives. Next day the corpses are covered up with whatever's to hand, a week later it's a distant memory. The nowness and the newness is what counts, eh? Sod the past, that's before your time. The Easter Rising? Detumescent, old sport. We don't need history in The Dump. A curious place. Sometimes a cry of "AEROSTAT!" The newcomers are baffled, interested, expectant. Whereas the old-timers have long since passed through these dangerous emotions. The old-timers know what to do. They scurry. Dive into ditches. Batten down the hatches. Retire to their sleeping bags with a good read. A manual on seamanship, say. Useful pictures of badges. Essential to avoid the embarrassment of confusing the masseur with the X-Ray assistant, the Chief Stoker with a sick berth attendant. Or a copy of – with hey, ho, the wind and the rain! – *King Lear*. Or a music magazine containing the true story of Jerry Lee Lewis's right leg and Roy Acuff's Yo-Yo. Or *The Annotated Baseball Stories of Ring W. Lardner 1914-1919*, describing real teams, real players and real situations in the real world of early major league baseball together with 111 illustrations of real ball players, real teams, real ball parks, newspaper items, and other memorabilia of one of the most fascinating and eventful eras in baseball history! Or a well-thumbed copy of *Mambo* ("Dynamic, pacy and full of unexpected twists" – *Scotland on Sunday*). Or O'Kill's *Window on the World*. Obasanjo's *My Command*. Or a fat book full of the gibbers (If we CONFESS our SINS, he is faithful and just to FORGIVE US our sins and to CLEANSE US from all unrighteousness – that sort of gibber). Or the delightful

Heinemann Educational Books edition of *Gulliver's Travels* – very popular in the remnants of Empire, you know – with the refreshing italicised verso note, *A number of passages which might be considered offensive have been omitted from this edition.* The Dump, yes. Eight hundred square miles of garbage. A tip, literally. Prone to leaching – squelch! chemical whiffs! nothing-to-worry-about-says-the-man-from-the-ministry – a.k.a. the contamination of the tip's environs by the motion of its pollutants underground. Prone to the odd lively explosion of trapped methane gas. Prone to sudden subsidence. Heap upon heap of piled rubbish. Some glistening with a lively putrefaction, some decaying with a quiet dignity as if in snug retirement in placid Bournemouth. Some luridly ablaze. Place of perfumes, stenches. The sweet reek of rotting vegetable waste. The toxic throat-tickling stink of burning polystyrene. And here and there a stark Proustian chassis triggers the imaginary odour of exhaust fumes on a crisp bright winter's morn, memories of a long line of boxed commuters, fingers drumming impatiently on the steering wheel while the grey-blue drifts puff out from their throbbing rears, the nitrogen dioxide swathing passing pedestrians and cyclists, then rising, rising, putting a delicate haze across the entire city, pleasantly reminiscent of the art of Caspar David Friedrich. Many abandoned tyres, newspapers and rags, good for keeping the population warm at night. A dirty jam jar glinting in the sunlight, clear and keen and marvellously bright. Thistles and grass. Smouldering sacks. Ash. No double-glazing (Dostoevsky wouldn't have liked it here). Smashed glass, broken frames. Paper cups. Thousands of empty cans. Ash. I WALKED FOR HOURS THAT DAY. One morning... I suppose if I am honest I always knew about The Dump and like everyone else said nothing, did nothing. After all, what can one person on their own do about The Dump? Nothing. Correction. Some people did mention it. Mother, for example. Once or twice in her long lifetime. Before her eyes went. Poor dears, I remember her saying once. And once: it's a crying shame. And upon another occasion, a day of tempest and storm: something should be done about it, it really should. And what is ever done about? I will tell you. Nothing. No one ever thinks they will find themselves in The Dump. I was like everyone else. Never in a million years did I expect to find myself living in The Dump. Trapped there. Unable to escape. If you had said such a thing to me before it happened I would have said you were bonkers. Stark staring. What happened? How did you get here? Over the barrier. Were rotor blades involved? Jet propulsion? A rocket, a capsule, a parachute? New arrivals are always put through the hoops by the old-timers. Such interest! Such enthusiasm! Before lapsing back into their usual apathy. The Old-Timers forget. They have lived in The Dump so long they barely remember the old world, let alone how they voyaged from there to here. They forget the disorientation, the confusion. But I am still young enough to remember. It. Was. Like. This. One morning I woke up and found myself lying on a wet, dirty mattress, in the midst of an enormous region of waste, desolation and burning rubbish. I don't mind admitting I was nonplussed. In fact to be honest it came as a bit of a shock. In fact more than a bit, to be honest. A quite considerable shock. A very great shock. I was stunned. I felt perturbation within my sphincter, a boiling surging liquidy panic. Quick as a flash I exerted muscular control. Phew! A close one. I suppose many people would have been a little down in the dumps so to speak to find themselves down there (here) in The Dump but not yours truly. I said to myself, every cloud has a silver lining. And do you know what? I'd never spoken a truer word. By a stroke of great good fortune I discovered that although my bedroom, my home, mother, all of Attlee Tower, all of Walthamstow, and all of London, had vanished, my pyjamas hadn't. It was good to know that although something very odd had happened I was still decent. At first I could hardly begin to imagine what had happened. I'd gone to bed the night before in the usual way, put out the light, and gone to sleep in my room with its familiar objects (model Lancaster bomber hanging from the ceiling; Leyton Orient poster; souvenir anchor from H.M.S. Victory; the little glass lighthouse from Alum Bay, with its layers of coloured sand). Now everything was gone. I was particularly upset to have lost my glass lighthouse, my Lancaster and mother. I was also puzzled. My first thought was that there had been an overnight nuclear war and London had been zapped by the enemy. But that didn't explain how I'd survived when everything and everyone else had apparently been vaporized. The flat mother and I lived in was on the top floor of Attlee Tower. How anyone could survive falling from the top floor in the middle of a nuclear war was a bit of a teaser. I decided I must have just been lucky. It must have been one of those freak occurrences which very occasionally happen. I seemed to remember once reading about someone who slipped off the top of a mountain and fell, landing at the bottom with nothing more than a few bruises and a twisted ankle. Not to mention all those people you keep hearing about who open the wrong doors in aircraft flying at five-thousand feet and land unharmed in haystacks. And the people buried alive in earthquakes who are dug out of the rubble thirteen days later, none the worse for wear apart from superficial bruising and a yearning for pint after pint of cool water. But it was no time to be worrying about the whys and wherefores. The main thing was I was stranded in the middle of a vast plain of ruin and desolation, and it was time to get out of there double quick. Ten to one it was radioactive, all the more reason to scarper sharpish. I didn't want trouble with my teeth, or sores, or anything like that. The only problem was, which direction to take? Everywhere I looked looked much the same. Emptiness, desolation, rubbish, fires burning here and there. Drifts of oily black smoke. I wasn't even sure whether I was in the middle of the ruins of my old home or whether I had been hurled through the air for several hundred yards (or even a mile), before landing by great good fortune on a mattress. In the end I decided to walk in what I hoped was the direction of the Town Hall. If there had been a nuclear war the people at the Town Hall would know what to do. They were probably already handing out application forms and mugs of soup and fresh pairs of underpants. I would need to hurry if I wasn't to miss out. Re-knotting the cord which held up my pale blue pyjama bottoms I set off briskly through the ruins. I hadn't gone very far before I stopped. Unfortunately my carpet slippers had vanished in the holocaust and it was painful walking in bare feet. There seemed to be broken glass everywhere, and already I had quite a nasty cut on one of my big toes. I was also cold and beginning to shiver. Before I went any further I decided I needed to find something more to put on. There were several bulging black rubbish sacks scattered around. I broke them open and began poking around inside. It must have been my lucky day because it wasn't long before I'd come across a very nice pair of grey trousers, a string vest, a white Marks and Spencer shirt with stylish blue stripes, a pair of matching grey socks and a pair of carpet slippers. They weren't one-hundred-per-cent what I was after (the trousers had a 36 waist and were far too big, the vest had chunks missing, the shirt was stained with green paint, the socks had holes in and the slippers were a faded fluffy pink and for a woman) but beggars can't be choosers. If I'd happened to meet anyone who knew me I would have felt like a proper charlie, but fortunately there wasn't a sign of life anywhere. I was a little apprehensive what might happen when I got back to civilisation. I didn't want to get arrested as a tramp. But I decided to cross that bridge when I came to it. I walked for hours that day, becoming increasingly despondent. It's slow-going in carpet slippers and baggy trousers, I can tell you. I was also hungry, thirsty and growing worried at the way the ruins just seemed to go on and on and on. I kept expecting to see scorched trees on the horizon, or undamaged buildings, or perhaps a patrol aircraft looking for survivors. Instead of which: nothing. Once, pulse quickening, I heard *Finlandia*'s life-enhancing thump and rattle. I glanced round in excited anticipation of a nearby orchestra. No go. Just the tinny mockery of my interminable tinnitus. Just more miles of waste and smoke and fire and rubbish and ship models from 1925. And bottles, bottles, bottles. Bottles everywhere. More even than used to lurk in mother's cupboard under the stairs and out in the yard and in the dark oily corners of the underground garage. As the day wore on I grew more and more puzzled about the ruins. I had expected to find the remains of roads and buildings. I even thought I might find other survivors, who might be able to tell me what had happened. But not only was there no one else around, the ruins increasingly seemed to resemble less the remains of a bombed city than a municipal rubbish dump. I couldn't understand why there were so many black sacks of rubbish everywhere. There must have been thousands of them. If there had been a nuclear attack surely the plastic sacks would have melted? And why were there so many cardboard boxes and packing cases and heaps of garden cuttings? Why were there piles of tyres? Why had the abandoned cars been stripped of their wheels? I walked and walked and walked, and then I hobbled and hobbled and hobbled. I could feel the blisters bubbling up on the soles of my feet. One of them had burst and hurt like hell. I was beginning to feel cold again, and hungry. Worse, the day was ending. The afternoon was finished. It was dusk. I sat down on a tractor tyre and began to cry. Having begun, I continued. By the middle I was worn out but I forced myself on to the end, ending with a sob, a whimper, a whisper. "Mother!" But mother said nothing. Mother was far, far away. It was not mother's voice which responded but another's. "O my back, my shoulders!" Cried the voice. Making me jump. The voice adding: "Overturn! Overturn! Overturn!" Oppressed by gravity I returned to planet earth after my small jump of surprise, turned, and scanned the wilderness. I saw at once a stranger. An outlandish figure in a red dressing gown. Standing up, I balanced myself on the tyre. This put me a good half metre above the surface of the all-encompassing desolation. My sense of ontological well-being, which had sunk to zero, went up a notch or two. "O my back, my shoulders!" the stranger said again, strangely. He was fifty metres away, standing on the summit of a heap of crates, sacks and old newspapers, examining me through a telescope. About the same age as me, I guessed. Early twenties. His back and shoulders looked okay to me. He had a goatee beard and was wearing glasses. And a red corduroy cap. And red shoes with red socks. His hands were as soft as a goat's belly. He looked like a nutter but beggars can't be choosers. "Help!" I called. "I'm lost. Can you tell me the way out of here?" He finished his examination of me and slipped the telescope into a red shoulder bag he was carrying. "Stranger in these parts, are we?" he called across to me. "Looking for the way to San Jose?" "That's right," I said, responding not to his second question. "I'm from Walthamstow. To tell you the truth I'm not even sure how I got here. I went to bed last night in the usual way and when I woke up I was here. Perhaps there's been a gas explosion. Have you seen today's news?" "The news! Ha ha! Very good. Yes, I have seen the news. Tomorrow's news and today's news and most of all, yesterday's news." "And was there a gas explosion? Any dead? My mother –". "Your mother is almost certainly alive." "Thank God," I ejaculated. He gave me a wan smile and, soon afterwards, a packet of Salt & Malt Vinegar Flavour Fine Crinkle Crisps. "I'm Leo," he said, descending from his heap. "I am as isolated as you could wish me to be," he continued. With indescribable composure. Making his way cautiously towards me. Adding: "I'm a socialist." "Very nice I'm sure," I said politely. A socialist, eh? I knew about people like Leo from the papers and TV. Dinosaurs, they were often called. People sadly out of date. Like balding middle-aged men with wisps of long greying hair and bell-bottom trousers, still thinking they were living in the swinging sixties. Pathetic. Socialism was dead, everybody knew that. It hadn't worked in Russia, it was a complete disaster. Not to mention the nationalised industries, all the bureaucracy. "I'm Jack," I lied. "Jack Robinson." "Have some crisps, Jack." "Thanks," I said, tearing open the packet and munching greedily. They tasted stale but I didn't care. I was ravenous. Strangely, for a socialist, Leo was my own age. In his late twenties. Not middle-aged at all. Curious. "Hence the red," Leo explained. He gestured at his dressing gown, his slippers. To underline the point he removed his cap, tossed it twirlingly into the air, and expertly caught it. (I had the impression he had done this lots of times before.) "I have a red flag in here," he continued, indicating his bag. "But as yet I have found no use for it. The prevailing mood in The Dump is largely one of apathetic acceptance of the state of things. There is anger, yes. There are periodic outbursts of rage. There is a widespread feeling of frustration and a longing for better times. But channeling these feelings into a fightback. Aye, there's the rub." He emitted an attenuated sigh seventeen seconds in duration, a sigh which I subsequently recognised as stemming from a complex melancholy of the sort which hinders concoction, refrigerates the heart, takes away stomach, colour and sleep, thickens the blood, contaminates the spirits, overthrows the natural heat, perverts the good estate of body and mind, and makes you weary of life itself until you cry out, howl and roar for the very anguish of your soul. Subsequently? Five years later. I lie. Ten. Twenty. When I had an education. Not then. Not upon first arrival, a time when my consciousness was a thin, weak patchwork of received prejudices, when my vocabulary was risible, my formulations orthodox, my opinions fourth rate, my experiences limited, my mind barely born. But Leo did not howl and roar, no. Terminating his sigh he shivered and tightened the belt of his dressing gown. "Ah well," he said. "Pessimism of the intellect, optimism of the will. Eh?" Not having a clue I simply grunted. A reaction which seemed to satisfy him. "Overturn! Overturn! Overturn!" he said next, incomprehensibly. Adding: "O my back, my shoulders! O Tythes, Excise, Taxes, Pollings, etcetera!" I decided to ignore his baffling outbursts. Besides, I had other things on my mind. The whereabouts of mother. My own whereabouts. What had happened to Walthamstow. What to do with the empty crisp packet. I felt quite stressed with all these matters pressing down on me. I looked round for a litter bin and seeing none stuffed the empty packet into my pyjama trousers. Observing my hesitation and consequent stuffing Leo said, "What did you do that for?" "Mother brought me up to be tidy," I explained. "If there is no litter bin always take your rubbish home with you. That is her creed." "For crying out loud!" Leo bellowed. "You are now a native of The Dump! You are living on a rubbish tip! You are swimming in a sea of waste, afloat upon a scum of droppings! What fucking difference do you think your fucking crisp packet makes?" "You want to watch your language," I said. "You'll learn," Leo retorted bitterly. "You'll learn. You are trapped here. A prisoner. And there is only one way out." "A prisoner?" "You'll find out. This is the place of castouts. Animal, vegetable and mineral. And human. Don't pretend. You always knew, didn't you? Everybody out there knows about The Dump. They just don't think it has anything to do with them. They cannot imagine it will one day happen to them. So people are happy to go on with their busy busy busy lives. Ah, always so busy! Ah, the shopping! The new settee! Ah, the radiant Chopin performance! Sport! The equaliser! The £8 million sponsorship deal! Fashion! Frosted rainbow colours! Taut stretchy satin! The black and white fine check jacket and matching calf-length skirt! Prada leather bags! The latest Annie Lennox album! The chocolate creams! The vermouth on the rocks! The Irish coffee! The new movie! The week's TV! The new exhibition! The rendezvous at the pub! The excellent restaurant! Motoring! The mould-breaking MGF with four-cylinder engine mounted behind the cockpit providing race-car balance, traction and light steering! The personalized numberplate! Exotic travel! The 700 islands of the Bahamas! Turkey! Israel! Indonesia! Gorgeous sun-drenched beaches and a harbour ringed with lush volcanic hills! Or nearer home, special 'Saver Sailings', duty-free shops and luxurious cruise-ferries which land you in civilised ports! The universally acclaimed – brilliantly imaginative, an astonishing compassion and honesty, sheer exuberance, enormous talent, staggering genius, a knockout – novel! Cooking! Salmon in pastry with hollandaise sauce! Duck à l'orange! Hot chocolate soufflé! Sex! Femoral intercourse! Ligottage! Feuille de rose! And later? The bergenias, the Michaelmas daisies, the hellebores! The day trip to Paris, the weekend break in Cromer, the ten days in Barcelona, the fortnight on Mykonos, the month in Nepal! The property pages! The charming and picturesque detached barn conversion situated on the outskirts of the historic village in an area of outstanding natural beauty with Hamstone fireplace, fitted country-style kitchen, oil fired central heating, sun lounge and paved patio, with double garage and attractive terraced garden, only one mile from the sea, with views of the bay!" "What do you mean, Out There?" I said. "Beyond The Barrier," he retorted. "The Barrier?" I said. "If we all held hands and rushed at The Barrier together it would fall. That's the only way. It's happened before and it will happen again. It will happen here, too. Perhaps you will be the nucleus of a new fightback. The harbinger of the upturn, so to speak." "I don't understand," I said. "You will," said Leo grimly. "You will. When you do I'll be in touch." Saying which, he hopped away. "Hey! Don't go away! At least tell me the way out of here!" Leo halted. Turned. He pointed east. "That way," he said, pointing north. "That way," he said, pointing south. "That way," he said, pointing west. "That way," he said. "Any bloody way. They all lead to the The Barrier." "I don't understand," I said. "Circummured," he whispered. Then winked. "How I abhor circularity!" he cried. And rushed off. He moved with a surprising agility, hopping, then skipping, then dancing a jig. From a hitherto non-existent pocket he produced a previously imaginary harmonica which he materialised by dint of dialectics and the power of positive thinking. Upon it he played as he jigged a jaunty "British Grenadier". Leo's dressing gown flapped around his smeared calves and helped pack another sentence into my tale. In a minute or so he was lost to sight, obscured behind drifts of smoke and the darkness of the coming night. I sat down again on the tractor tyre for a think, always a good thing to do in moments of stress. But my mind was a clutter of panics and worries. It was really quite idiotic, blundering about in a rubbish dump all day. The sundry and the fiery! Probably I was just going round in circles all the time, like characters do in desert movies. In the end I decided to climb the heap recently vacated by Leo. I needed urgently to locate my bearings (not to mention my balls, which, when I'd found them, I scratched vigorously). I half hoped that from the top I'd catch a glimpse of the Town Hall, or maybe even Attlee Tower itself. No such luck. All I could see through the drifts of smoke and the growing darkness was heaps of piled rubbish. Rotting vegetable waste. Here and there a rusting chassis, an abandoned tyre, a dirty jam jar glinting in the sunlight. Thistles and grass, smouldering sacks, ash, thousands of empty cans. Trash, waste, rubbish, crap, in every direction, as far as the horizon. It began to rain. Half-heartedly. A few pelting drops. I shivered. I was beginning to feel cold and hungry and very thirsty. I descended Leo's heap and explored the lower slopes, tearing open rubbish sacks with a stick. Twenty minutes of brisk foraging uncovered a smelly tartan blanket, some lengths of worn, dusty, green carpet, some plastic sheeting, a bottle of flat lemonade and a packet of soft digestive biscuits. I decided it was enough to keep body and soul together until the next day. By a stroke of good fortune of the sort often found in picaresque narratives I found a delightful only-recently-scooped trench concealed beneath the sacks. It was six metres long, a couple of metres deep. No one had vomited or defecated there and the trench had a not entirely unpleasant odour of fresh earth. I re-arranged the sacks to conceal my presence from any wandering predator (mutant ants and prowling carnivores came looking for me in that chink of my mind where old movies shimmered in the heat-haze of blind panic). I then jumped down into the trench and wrapped myself in the blanket and strips of carpet. Lastly I spread the plastic sheeting over me. Nibbling the biscuits and sipping the sweet lemonade made me think of my childhood. I suddenly remembered how I used to pretend my bed was a submarine, and I'd crawl under the sheets in the dark and nibble a biscuit, pretending I was on the sea-bed, with depth charges crashing all around. That first night I didn't sleep a wink. I wondered about the books which Leo kept in his bag. *Theories of Surplus Value. The Getaway. William – The Outlaw.* It was so cold, so very, very cold. I was also somewhat disturbed by the strange circumstances in which I found myself. I'd no sooner nod off than I'd wake, thinking of mother, and Walthamstow, and my life up to that moment. You see I was born and brought up in Walthamstow. To be more precise, I was born in Thorpe Coombe Hospital on Forest Road, not far from the Town Hall. The Hospital isn't used for deliveries anymore. In fact the only times I've been back since being born there was to see the nurse about my head lice. Walthamstow is divided into three parts (though this is not on any maps and only the natives know it). There is Upper Walthamstow, where the well-off bastards live with drive, garage, two cars, four bedrooms and a lav downstairs as well as up. There is South Walthamstow, which is where the poor and the transients live, in maisonettes and council flats. South Walthamstow has rubbish blowing about the streets and graffiti and cracked pavements. Then there is The Rest of Walthamstow, which is where the not-desperately-poor-but-not-exactly-rich live in little two-bedroom houses with poky gardens containing manhole-sized squares of concrete called "the patio." This pattern is part of a bigger pattern. To the north is Chingford and Wanstead, where even bigger, richer bastards live. I've been once or twice, you wouldn't believe it, some of the houses out there. Fucking enormous detached houses with fucking enormous drives and triple garages with remote-control doors and Porsches on the gravel and their own fucking LAMPPOSTS in the front garden. But the other way, via Walthamstow, you move in the opposite fiscal direction. First you encounter bleak Leytonstone and bleaker Leyton, and then it gets even worse and you hit treeless soul-less traffic-jammed Stratford, horrible. But I digress. I suppose like everyone else I thought one day I'd shack up with someone and have a couple of kids and feed them nourishing supermarket baby food containing chalk, animal intestines, pig's feet, cotton waste and glue, like everyone else, and one day retire to a jerry-built bungalow at the oil-and-sewage-oozing sea-side. Something along those lines. My life up to the age of thirty-one uneventful. I barely remember it. My thirty-second year a complete blank. My thirty-third evoking no delusions that I was the Son of God or A Man With A Mission. My thirty-fourth risible, my thirty-fifth humiliating, my thirty-sixth dull beyond words. All dull beyond words. I ache to get there, beyond all this, this spiky painful trash, these endless rectangles of language, these symmetrical lines banal as humming pylons on a rainswept prairie. I grew up, stunted and enfeebled, in South Walthamstow, needless to. To say. I played on the rusty broken swings in the bleak puddled playground next to Attlee's dark Tower, I suppose. I hit my sister, I suppose. Sister? Grete? Drugs alcohol little sister bang! bang! I was pushed over and cut my knees and bled copiously and wept bitterly, I suppose. One of my earliest memories is trying to put a model aeroplane together. A Spitfire. I got as far as putting the fuselage together and attaching the cockpit, then I discovered how nice the glue smelled. Later I ate too much egg and chips and was sick. I set fire to the Spitfire in the sandpit. It burned beautifully. Thick black oily smoke, big yellow flames. I remember tenderly my arson phase. I just couldn't stop burning things. First it was books and clothes, then I learned plastic burned brightest, burned best. A bucket, then an abandoned traffic cone in the street. Once I even stuffed lots of paper and cardboard under somebody's old Rover in the underground car park. The car didn't have a petrol cap. Next day two policemen came knocking at the door, asking where I'd been at the time of the explosion. Mother swore I was in watching a video. "What video?" they snapped, faces twisted by suspicion. Mother retorted, it was all she could think of, "*Oklahoma!*" Snorted they! Believed her they did not! Much to go on obviously did they not have, apart from a vague description of a mucky nondescript boy. Luckily I am the mundane distilled into human form. I am the grey quintessence of the banal. I am a zero, a nothing, a dull bubble. I have no distinguishing characteristics. People do not remember me. My memory is poor. My past is a featureless grey plain wiped clean by the drip-drip-drip of the cold years. When the imaginary police had gone my imaginary mother looked suspiciously at her imaginary son and did not say: "Were you involved, Raymond?" "Stupid cow!" I screamed. "I was Raymond in the first draft. I'm Jack now, and likely to remain so until this Ivor is well and truly wrapped up." Ivor? Novella! Sorry. "Were you involved, dear Jack?" "Of course not, gentle mother." No. I am like sweet Jesus. Not once in my life have I succumbed to filthy temptation. Never, never, never have I wedged a fingernail inside either of my nostrils in order to scrape off a lump of hardened mucus. Never have the empurpled, swollen, unwholesome lips of my crusted anus bulged outward, forming a knobbly nought and let rip a screeching, bubbling stinking jet of intestinal gas. Never once have I fondled my private parts in a shameful quest for sensual delight. Nor the parts of others, irrespective of gender. Never have I pissed anywhere but in local authority urinals and other approved china receptacles. Never have I defecated into a coronation mug, or into a bowl celebrating a royal wedding, or among ferns. I have led a clean, simple, honest, decent life, in consequence of which I have been made redundant. Off to The Dump with him! Funnily enough I could see The Dump from my very earliest days. Pressing my snub nose against the window. Focusing on the misty distances. Strange now to think that The Dump was actually visible from our flat on the top storey of Attlee Tower. The Dump was (is!) only a couple of miles away to the south-west, at the Borough borders. As I said, Attlee Tower is in South Walthamstow, as I didn't say, not far from St James Street Station. Attlee Tower was built in 1966. It is flanked by Gaitskell Tower and Bevan Tower, built at the same time. The towers are named after famous people. Gaitskell and Bevan were both important Labour politicians who died unexpectedly. Attlee Tower is named after Clem Attlee. I do not know much about him except that he was a very famous socialist and was once the MP for West Walthamstow, in the old days. The Golden Days of the Attlee Government, as mother called them. (Leo, by the way, says this is complete balls, and that Attlee was a class traitor and a shit.) From the twenty-fourth floor of Attlee Tower you get a lovely view of the deracinated highway-slashed wastes of Epping Forest in the north and the bleak, banal Lea Valley in the south. Walthamstow is in the middle, like a slice of mouldy cheese between two stale slices of bread. In my experience everyone has heard of Walthamstow E17. It has quite a history. Talk about Dan Bartholemew's Dolorous Discourses! Associations include Byron (reputed – exact site unknown – to have passed a debauched night with Claire Clairmont in one of the terraced houses on Byron Road, returning some years later for a solitary night with Madame S------ and penning stanza 41 of Canto IX of *Don Juan*), Milton (widely believed to have penned one or two lines of his immortal *Paranoid List* in the old police flats now known as Milton House, on Milton Road) and of course William Morris, the very talented wallpaper designer, who lived as a child in a demolished house opposite the fire station. Later his parents moved to the William Morris Gallery just up the road. And of course the world famous pop group. Mention must also be made of the mysterious building on Markhouse Road, bearing the inscription MARX HOUSE 1884. Leo reckons it was where Karl Marx's grieving daughters moved after the old man's death. He has a theory that the road was once Marx House Road and that the name was changed years ago when the Tories grabbed control of the Council. You must admit it sounds plausible. Moreover, as Ellis noted, Eleanor Marx knew William Morris, and as Kapp observes Ellis is very widely accepted as an authority, therefore it must be true, as anyone with no axe to grind must surely see. From our flat in Attlee Tower mother and I had a perfect view of The Dump. Or as perfect as anyone can get without flying over in a balloon or helicopter (and until Shocking Events Unfolded I had never appreciated the significance of the regular passage of balloons up and down the Lea Valley, or the interminable ever-present police helicopter circling Walthamstow). The Dump is the municipal tip. Exclusive to the London Borough of Waltham Forest. The place where the rubbish men used to take their vehicles until they opened the flash waste disposal unit at Edmonton. The place where rubbish has been dumped since the beginning of time (or at any rate since the beginning of the twentieth century). The place where people are encouraged to take their sacks of garden refuse and unwanted newspapers and other unwanted domestic material. To get to The Dump just take the road past St James's Park and continue. Keep right on to the end of the road, as that Scotchman sings. You can't miss it. There's a tall wire fence with a security gate and behind it portakabins and parked vans. In the middle distance, the waste incinerators, low, grey, obscure buildings with a single tall chimney belching clouds of thick black boiling smoke. In the far distance, a paler, bluer smoke from burning refuse and a vast bank of rubbish bearing a strong resemblance to the serpentine earthworks of Maiden Castle seen from the Dorchester by-pass. Follow the fence until you come to an open entrance. Here there's a sort of lay-by, where you can pull in with your car or van and lug your rubbish over to a row of open refuse containers each the size of a single-decker bus. One for metals, one for wood, one for tyres, one for garden rubbish, one for paper. And three bottle banks in orthodox colours (white, brown, green). The lay-by is a smelly, dirty, rubbish-strewn place and you just go in, do the business, and get out fast. Away through the exit and back up the road to Walthamstow. Easy peasy. It's not the kind of place anyone would choose to linger. If you bothered to look beyond the refuse containers – nobody does, of course – you would see dirty once-yellow bulldozers piling up garbage against a vast bank of refuse.

The atmosphere around The Dump is foul. It reeks. Putrefaction layered with strong, toxic whiffs. A raw, vegetable stench. The stink of sodden brown rotting grass blended with a thousand decaying cabbages. With an added tang of burning rubber and polystyrene. Stay more than five minutes and you'd need a gas mask. At least that's what I thought then. Little did I know... I sometimes wonder if the air pollution and general stink is done deliberately, to discourage public interest. Fires burn night and day around the perimeter of The Dump, casting a perpetual pall of smoke over it. Serving a double purpose, perhaps? To discourage public interest AND to obscure and render opaque what is actually GOING ON in The Dump? It is certainly the case that though we knew The Dump was there and though we could see it from Attlee Tower, we never really saw it CLEARLY. In that respect it was just like Nessie. There was always smoke drifting here and there, blocking the view. We saw the people, of course, I can't pretend we didn't. But it was easy to pass them off as refuse workers or investigative policemen searching for blood-smeared dismembered limbs or idle scavengers who shunned a hard day's work. It makes me sick to think about it. EVERYBODY FUCKING KNOWS ABOUT THE DUMP BUT NOBODY FUCKING CARES! Sorry. My apologies for that little outburst. I detest polemical fiction as much as the next man. Narrative should never be fouled by propaganda or pastiche or a plurality of contradictory discourses but should refresh the mind and enlarge the reader's moral being through the subtle evocation of bourgeois anxieties. Shit like *The Princess Casamassima*, eh? Verisimilitude, eh? And the smell! I can't pretend we never smelled it. I can't pretend our nostrils were never assailed by the thick tidal stench of faeces and rotting weed and worse which seemed to linger on every street, not to mention in the lifts. And everyone could smell it but no one ever talked about it. Even on the days when the Department of the Environment said the air quality was "very exceptionally nice". All that long first night I tossed and turned in my trench. I hadn't known it was possible to be so cold. I shivered and turned and twisted and twitched and tried to make myself comfortable. Couldn't sleep a wink. I cast my mind back to my dreary past. I cast it forward to my rescue. My rescue! The only survivor of the great Walthamstow gas explosion! The helicopter hovering overhead in response to my desperate semaphore appeals! Rushed away by stretcher under the blaze of TV lights, my heart beating like the fanners of a mill. A miraculous escape! Selling my story to the *News of the World*. Fifty grand's worth! I was made! Such fantasies, I learned, are commonplace among the new arrivals. Fantasies soon shattered by the reality of The Dump. Fantasies ended by The Barrier. By the aerostats. By the whole caboodle. Fast asleep? No. Slow awake. The slowest wake of all. Cold as death. Hell. I woke up, no, I was never asleep. Did I doze? Possibly. I do not remember dozing, mind. I became aware of different shades of darkness, of night's candles burned out, of the morning, grey as sludge. Of rain, pitter-pattering on the rubbish sacks, on my plastic sheeting. The sheets were covered in condensation, I was all damp and sweaty, I felt terrible, hungry, thirsty, you name it. I didn't even have the energy to climb out of the trench for a piss, just kneeled, unzipped and splattered the end where my feet were. Some went on my socks, hitherto unmentioned. A very nice pair of Marks and Spencer grey cotton. The rain came down in torrents. Bucketing down, so to speak. I ate my last two biscuits, drank the last of the flat lemonade. I often read in novels about people pinching themselves to make sure they aren't in a dream, so I pinched myself. Didn't feel a thing! But it didn't mean I was in a dream, did it? All it fucking meant was that I was numb with cold, that's bloody what. Bloody stupid idea, pinching yourself. Bruising your own skin to prove some fatuous point about reality. Bloody bloody bloody stupid. In any case The Dump isn't a dream, it's more like a fucking nightmare. Sorry. Excuse language. I've been feeling under a lot of stress lately. Like for example the past twenty-five years. Sorry. I'll try and pull my socks up. Or I would do, if I had any. But I haven't. (At least not in the first draft. Once you get on to the second and third drafts things start to change, it's all very disturbing.) There are those who argue that This Is Like Life – unexpected events, trees crashing down in the night, earthquakes – and those who argue that this is merely The Fictiveness of

Fiction. And then again there are those, the vast majority, who have no interest in these matters at all, largely because they are ill, or dying, or more interested in sport, or needing to complete a treatise on heterophony by Tuesday or too busy practising on a violino grande Penderecki's immortal concerto or gnawed by Angst or far too tied up in overseeing the deployment of sonar equipment and skilled operators employing both fixed station and mobile modes of operation and using both low and high resolution systems ranging from 20kHz to 250kHz in frequencies in the ongoing search for a large unknown animal in Loch Ness. I prayed. At once the rain stopped. I drew no conclusions. I was not in the mood for drawing anything. I went back to the top of the heap. My hair had grown longish and I ran my hands through it till it stood up like a cockatoo's crest. I began to think that I should split in two. The croaking of the frogs by the Labongo sounded in my brain. I remembered the path up the Berg and the groves of stinkwood. I gazed at the surrounding rubbish. It was covered with rime and slime. I felt a prickling sense of unease. It seemed different somehow. I tried to remember how it had looked yesterday and what it was that had changed, but couldn't. It was just... different. I couldn't see a soul. Fires were still burning, despite all the rain. I decided to follow the direction Leo had gone in. One way looked as good as another. Pulling up my socks from the second draft I set off. I sincerely hoped they would not be removed from me in a subsequent draft. So far so good. Noon, probably. A couple of waste hours elapse, I suppose. Two o'clock, must be. Everything is different but just the same. Different pillars of flame and burning tyres and smoke. Different heaps of rubbish. Different broken glass. But basically all just the same bloody mess as before. Christ, I've had enough. Tired. Thirsty. Feeling out of sorts. A bit peckish. I poked about in some bags and found a jam doughnut. Rock hard. Greedily I licked off the sugar. I hurt my teeth when I tried to bite into the doughnut. In the end I managed to moisten and eat most of it. With a swig of Lucozade for refreshment, the few last golden drops in an old bottle. Very possibly 5 p.m. Can't take much more of this. Exhausted. Very hungry, very thirsty. I wish I could find Leo but there is no sign of him anywhere. 8 p.m. I expect. I came across the wardrobe as dusk fell. It lay on its side, the door missing. A perfect resting place for the night. I crawled inside and found a scrawl. *Plomer woz ear*. Eh? I made myself as comfortable as I could. In no time at all – and truly I had no time at all, my watch not having come with me to The Dump but still tick-tocking and gathering dust on the bedside table in Attlee Tower, hence the wild guesswork involved in the unreliable times given above – I was asleep. A good night's sleep! It is the sweetest thing. I slept a shagged-out sleep, like a lusty young fellow in du Maurier country, who thrice hath pleasured his fair young maiden on the secluded shoreline by Shag Rock, undisturbed by the huge snake which probably slithered over me in the night like in *Walkabout*. I woke to drips dripping on my face (which reminded me of the dying private dick at the end of *Blood Simple*), someone or thing had pissed on the wardrobe in the night. Mopping myself dry I crawled out, feeling the warmth of sunlight on my face. The sky was a bright blue. Somewhere nearby a bird was cheeping like an electronic game. In the night The Dump had changed again. I was certain of it. Once again I felt a prickling sense of unease. Something was different. Something. If only I could put my soiled finger on it. I rolled sideways across some enticing trash, I forget exactly what. Feathers? That morning was the morning my constipation would be over, I was certain of it. I slithered to the back of the wardrobe, slipped down my pyjamas and adopted a squatting posture. Out it came, a gorgeous glistening serpentine turd, curling itself up on the ground like a well-trained snake, of an admirable light brown colour with a firm consistent texture. I felt chirpy as that unidentifiable bird. Now all I had to do was get to grips with malnutrition, thirst, a sense of disorientation and the lack of a toothbrush. A razor and some shaving foam would come in handy, too, though I knew that if push came to shove I could get by with a beard. The battery inside the unseen bird went flat. I shrugged, like a character in a novel. A shrug! I regretted it at once. I had never before shrugged in my life. I found the experience unnatural and ridiculous. It seemed akin to a tic or a twitch. I knew I would never, ever, shrug again. A trickle of sweat made its way down my face, cleverly imitating the course of Amhuinn Caslaval. I felt suddenly grateful for the desolation and solitude. I had never seen anyone shrug in public before and now I knew why. People would laugh. I felt unclean. My mouth tasted foul, my teeth as if they were covered in fur. What I needed was a chuckling spring, a bubbling brook or even a muddy waterhole. Stupid, stupid, stupid! I'd clean forgotten. All that rain! There was water all around me, if only I'd thought of it earlier. There was rainwater gathered in the creases of the garbage sacks. There was rainwater in shallow pools in up-ended hub caps and old cracked sinks and plantpots and tin trays. I scooped the water and drank. I scooped the water and flushed out my mouth. I splashed it over my face, my uncombed, matted hair. Things were looking up! Do you know I even started to whistle! I began with "All I Have To Do Is Dream", moved on to "King Of The Road" and was in the middle of "I Love You Because" when there was a distant *crack!* and a bullet smacked into the rear of the wardrobe. Splinters of wood spat at my terror. The bullet passed through the wardrobe and went ricocheting among some old half-buried agricultural machinery, among the rusted, flaking blades and wheels of which grew primroses and daisies and a solitary blue hollyhock. Here, among stumps of thorn, the pale-eyed Dysdera, with jutting chelicerae, hunts the woodlouse, swinging her cephalothorax on one side, piercing her twice. I threw myself to the ground, which is easier said than done and also very painful. Fortunately I had barely bruised my kneecaps before a powerful force threw me upright, the bruises healed with Christ-like speed, and, vision obscured by a commonplace scarlet mist which must have blown in from a nearby crime thriller, I did not see the scattered splinters of chipboard swoop back and plug the bullet hole, the woodlouse detach itself from the spider and scurry backwards, or the bullet hurriedly retrace the zig-zag course of its ricochet before reversing at great speed into the distance, where the crack! of a rifle imploded into silence, a silence coinciding with the instant dismissal of the mist and broken only by my own merry whistling. I ended the Jim Reeves song and moved effortlessly into a jaunty rendition of "There Goes My Everything". I'd been hallucinating. Must have been LSD in the lemonade. An old trick. The thought of hallucinations was comforting. Almost anything and anywhere was better than The Dump, even my mind. But I didn't like being shot at, even if the bullets were illusory. Eh? Nonsense. I'd not been hallucinating. I simply hadn't grasped the complexity of the place, its geomorphology of waste paper and black holes. Pardon. I'm getting ahead of my self (as the gravemarked time traveller said to his fit, muscular double). Taking you back to those long-gone solitary night walks, the orange sodium street lights, your dwarf's shadow compressed beneath your size eleven shoes. As you walk away the shadow lengthens, elongates, distorts. You're a fool in a crazy mirror, your broken heart inside you like pieces of shrapnel. Ah such young man's similes, be off with you! Be off across the great wastes, all the dead time, the Sundays at the Kwara Hotel, drinking too much, listening to Kris Kristofferson singing "Sunday Morning Coming Down," the donkey braying amid the lines of parked cars, genial spirits failing, forlorn! Be off. In Leo's direction. In theory. Difficult to be sure, no landmarks. A persistent whiff of burning rubber, litter everywhere, did I mention all the paper, the polystyrene cups? And the flies. A bit of warmth and sunshine and out they poured, buzz buzz. Swarming excitedly over my glistening turd, like royal correspondents at a Prince's wedding, a Princess's funeral. Feasting on the soft grey growths dappling the erectile tissue of rotting carrots. Probing cancered oranges. Go away! Wasps, too. And the occasional plump bumbling bee. No sign of Leo anywhere, can't really say I'm surprised. Morning ended, the afternoon began, so I imagine. Clouding over now. The blotch of sun above roughly overhead, noon I suppose. All that afternoon I trudged and tramped, treading carefully, stepping over empty oxygen canisters and skeletons of tents, taking steps to avoid treading on any corpses or broken glass. Pausing occasionally to warm myself by one of the many blazing fires. The sun – Alexander is jubilant! – came out again from between some grey cloud and beamed down upon – Alex is dumbfounded – The Dump. Provoking fiery glints in specks of shattered bottle. And then. Something. Glimmering. In the Chinese distance. A distinct

46

glimmer, yes! Whatever it was it was well above the surface of The Dump. Bluish-grey. Like water. More cloud. End of sunbeams. End of glimmer. Trudged on, tired, thirsty, hungry, the usual. Thirst not so bad after discovering all the rainwater. The discovery some three hours and ten minutes ago of a packet of children's striped straws also came in very handy for sucking up quite small quantities of rainwater. Goody! More biscuits! Trudged on, humming an old Animals number appropriate to my situation. Aficionados will get my gist. On and on. On and on. On and on. Jesus! Trees! Green trees. Near the edge now, must be! Be soon out of this place! Laughter, feelings of good cheer! "Top o' the world t' ye!" Better than six pints of Greene King! Robinson breaks into a run, always a dangerous thing to do, falls flat on his face. A banana skin, yes. Picks himself up, brushes off the bits, ignores the slight gash on his left hand, continues running. Trees, six of them. Growing on a low grassy bank. Beyond... A fence. Jesus! A perimeter fence! An easily climbed wire mesh fence, not more than four metres high. A piece of cake. Curving round until lost in the distance. That must be what was glimmering in the distance. The Dump bigger than Robinson had realised. Not to worry, soon be out of here. The garbage ends, there's some grey ashy stuff, and then there's the fence. The way out! You can even see Walthamstow, the towers, houses, a distant yellow bulldozer. The end – tee hee! – of Alexander's ordeal! Bloody marvellous! You run towards it, of course. Like thousands before you. You jump over the last sack of rubbish, skip over an old newspaper, crunch a paper cup beneath your foot, run across the ash, miniature dustclouds rising up. ZAAAAAP! Without warning, a painful crackling over the surface of your body, a force slamming into your chest, something throwing you backwards – splatter – into a crate of rotting oranges. A few curls of smoke rising from your scorched clothing, a faint whiff of burning. You scramble to your feet, buttocks soaked in orange juice, bits of squashed orange slithering – shit! shit! shit! – down your inside thighs. Can't believe that it really happened, try again, a different spot this time, twenty metres to the left, very slowly, slowly, both hands stretched out, got to reach those trees, got to get out of this Christ-

awful place, Jesus, Mother, please God, no more tricks, no more –
ZAAAAAP! The same painful crackling, the same invisible fist
punching you, tossing you backwards again, this time against a
waste of old newspapers, wham! Where you lie winded, tears in
your eyes, sobbing with rage and frustration. Just a few fucking
yards and you'd be out of this fucking place! Fuck! Fuck! Fuck!
Some sort of invisible force field. The sort of thing you come
across in science fiction but not something you expect to find in
Walthamstow. Strange. You might have expected the fence to be
electrified but not an empty space. Some sort of invisible ray,
presumably. Strange, yes. The trees unmistakeably REAL. You
can even hear their leaves rustling in the gentle breeze. "Help!
Help!" You shout. "HELP! For Christ's sake! Please." Like
thousands before you. Waving frantically, hoping someone will
see you. The bulldozer driver, for example. Are you deaf and
blind, man? The people in the distant tower blocks. Doesn't
anyone have a pair of binoculars and a sense of curiosity and
concern? Jesus H. Christ! What's the world coming to? But no
one hears you, no one stirs, no one comes to your assistance. No
one will ever hear you. And so, in the end, like thousands before
you, you get to your feet. You have had (stand back) an idea.
Perhaps you can't get across the fence here but perhaps if you go
further along the perimeter you'll find a place where this doesn't
happen. By now the day is ending. Time to eat, drink, piss, brush
teeth and sleep. Goo'night. Zzzzzzz. Up bright and early, sun
shining brightly from a clear sky, wire fence gleaming, trees green
and flourishing, brisk brushing of teeth, a hearty breakfast, a
good, solid stool, and off you go, whistling a merry tune. "I Want
To Hold Your Hand," if I remember rightly. Which way? I
wondered. Left, I decided. Northward, if my sense of direction is
right. A brisk pace, the trees falling away behind, the tower blocks
gradually dropping from view, beyond the fence now nothing but
vacancy, waste lots, low distant buildings, a solitary chimney
belching thick black smoke, ghostly faraway figures, wagons,
containers heaped high with rubbish, litter blowing about
everywhere, gusts of smoke, the smell of burning plastic. Slowing,
casually stepping closer to the fence, I made a sudden dash

towards the wire. Seconds later I was lying among some ill-smelling sacks, with curls of blue smoke rising up from my pyjama trousers. Baffled, enraged, I moved on. All that day I tried rushing the fence, and each time I was hurled back into The Dump. At sunset I gave up, found a nice dry mattress and lay down and wept. I was so tired and bruised I would probably have fallen asleep at once, and in the first draft I closed my eyes and came tantalisingly close to enjoying a much-deserved fourteen-hour snooze, then a cold second draft blew in some changes. A clammy hand closed upon my shoulder and a voice said, "You new around here, son?" I opened my eyes and saw a silent mysterious saucer-shaped silver craft high in the sky, and, very much nearer, about six inches away in fact, an old man with long white hair and a beard, looking as if he had stepped out of a painting by William Blake. He had kindly, twinkly eyes. Like Leo, he was wearing a dressing gown (but this one was blue, not red). From the spacious pocket of his gown, where he kept his notebook, pencils, portable filing cabinet, butterfly net, foot pump, comb, magnifying glass, matches and copy of *Where Is Britain Going?* he produced a tangerine, which I gratefully guzzled. Beyond his left shoulder there was a sort of flash in the blue empyrean as the escaped weather balloon sped away to cause a scare over Canning Town. "People call me The Historian," he said. "Come and have some tea, you look tired. I expect you've had too many electric shocks today, eh? Been throwing yourself against The Barrier, have you?" Sheepishly I nodded, a trick I had learned two years earlier from the careful four-hour observation of a flock in Cumbria. He lived not far away in a concealed ditch, the old man. Rolling back a length of mildewed carpet, he beckoned me in. "There are steps," he explained, descending. I followed him down. "Have a seat," he said, indicating a comfy armchair covered with a familiar Morris floral print. Flicking off a slumbering earthworm, I sat down. He went to the far end of his cosy nook and lit an oil lamp. I heard the rattle of crockery, the splash of water, the soft hiss of a portable Gaz stove. A remarkable ditch! And so many books! They were piled in heaps on the floor and wedged tightly on shelves along the walls. Paperbacks, hardbacks, a few magazines. And over everything the rank raw smell of a freshly dug grave. It made a nice change from burning plastic. I extracted a volume, causing a miniature avalanche of earth. One of the pillars of bricks supporting the plank shelving swayed perilously. The book, a stout hardback, had a battered cover the colour of dried blood. A brownish stain had seeped along the upper edge of every page. The pages smelled as musty and unwell as a dying septuagenarian. "Aha," said the old man, returning from the far end of the ditch with some light refreshment, "I see you have dug out my little monograph on vertical looms. In the Vatican library there is a very old illustrated manuscript of Virgil's immortal *Aeneid* which depicts a wooden structure consisting of two uprights on feet connected by three equidistant horizontal bars with an irregular clear patch just above the lowest bar, the middle bar almost certainly representing the heddle rod, the structure as a whole almost certainly being that of fourth century A.D. upright loom in which the warp weights have already been replaced by a breast or cloth beam and the weaving begins from the bottom and not from the top. Rich tea or digestive?" "Digestive, please." "If you poke around you might find the companion volume on Oriental vertical mat looms. Though to be frank with you the entire topic of weaving, with its rods and leashes and beams and threads and sheds and warp and weft and spools and shuttles and bobbins bores me stiff. Give me a round table seminar on Herodotus any day, say, or even King Arthur, say, or Thucydides, say, or Bishop Jeremy Taylor's contention that 'he to whom all things are one, who draweth all things to one, and seeth all things in one, may enjoy true peace and rest of spirit', say, or Marx's argument that Trades Unions fail generally from limiting themselves to a guerrilla war against the effects of the existing system instead of simultaneously trying to change it by using their organised forces as a lever for the final emancipation of the working class, that is to say, the ultimate abolition of the wages system. Say." He put the tin tray down on a small coffee table. The coffee table surface mapped precipitation in Europe, the tin tray reproduced Gainsborough's portrait of Joshua Kirby, and the two steaming mugs of tea bore reproductions of *Oriolus oriolus oriolus* and *Bombycilla garrulus garrulus*. "Reykjavik and Bergen are places to avoid, eh?" he said with a wink. "Unless you like getting wet, that is." "I hate birds," I replied. "Stupid things. I've never seen the point in them." "Best steer clear of Reykjavik and Bergen, then, eh?" The old man chuckled. "I like your tray," I said. "If I am not mistaken it shows Joshua Kirby, editor of Brook Taylor's treatise on perspective. Buried in Kew churchyard, I believe." "I wouldn't know about that," he said tersely. "What I do know is that The Dump is a place of mysteries. But drink up, lad. Drink up thy tea." "Aye, aye, captain." My hands shook, and a slop of tea went all over the monograph on vertical looms. "Woops, sorry!" "Not to worry, lad. Not to worry. Like I said I frankly couldn't give a brass farthing. Another digestive?" "I think I'll try one of the rich tea, this time, thank you." Babbled he on as I munched, telling me that a fact is relative, and if placed out of its relative position, it apparently is not a fact, often, and that dialectics knows no hard and fast lines, and that a stone dropped from a train cannot be seen to move in a curve by any passenger but only by the woman on the embankment, and that the geo-centric system attributed to Ptolemy led to complications in the calculation of planetary orbits, and that there is only one cartouche on the hieroglyphic section of the slab of granitoid stone appropriated from Rashid by French troops in July 1799, and that the west wall at Chaldon church portrays a Descent into Limbo, the Torments of Hell, the Seven Deadly Sins, the Weighing of Souls, the Tree of Knowledge. "A spectrum is haunting Yggdrasil!" he whispered, giving me a fierce wink, speaking of space and Proust, of how the range of masses of the stars is one-eighth to twenty times the solar mass, of time and the cyclic dynamism of the intermediate, of Soddy and isotopes, of William Faulkner's unhappiness with *God is My Co-Pilot*, of the ionic theory of Svante Arrhenius and Baudelaire's "Chacun Sa Chimère", and of how caustic potash must be applied at once to the wounds of a person bitten by a deranged pug. Words, phrases, concepts rolled over me like huge soft velvet balls, pressing themselves against my brain, nudging and pummelling and teasing me. I felt sleepy and baffled and only half-awake. A dizziness seemed to steal over me, clouding my mind. At first I listened to nine words out of ten, but soon I was only half listening, then perhaps not listening at all, my mind full of feathers, of an eiderdown, of springy textual matrices, of mists and echoes. The old man explained how The Dump, though occupying only a tiny area of the Lea Valley, had a topography equivalent to that of a Middle Eastern desert, and how the population – and here I had a prickling confused sense that the old man was as mute as a hookah – was almost certainly in the thousands. "Tens of thousands!" he screeched, thumping the sludge with his stick. "Millions!" His stick? A blind man's white stick, materialising silently out of the all-encompassing blackness. With a black rubber ferrule. "Most of the population lives underground, only emerging at night," he confided in a voice like breaking crockery. "Millions?" I said. "Surely not." He nodded, then shook his head, then winced at the confused body movements he was being subjected to by forces outside his control. "The true figure will never be known," he added brokenly. "A proper statistical count is out of the question. The death rate is high. And there are regions where even an Historian does not go." By now it was evening. The Historian yawned and lit more candles. "Your beard!" I cried, dowsing the flame. "Thank you, my boy. At my age... One's faculties begin to wander. Little damage done, fortunately. A singed patch, shrivelled blackened hairs, nothing to write home about. A brief spasm of pain, then all over. More tea?" "Yes, please." That's better. Almost dark outside now. Now it is dark. "Come, my boy." The old man took the lantern and led me outside. He walked seven metres north-by-north-west, then pointed at the ground with his stick. "My guest ditch," he said. "Not very luxurious but you will find all the necessaries. Here, take this," he continued, handing me something wrapped in tissue. "Goodnight!" "Goodnight." His lantern receded. I turned my attention to the guest room. It resembled a shallow grave. I eased myself into the cramped musty-smelling space, pulled a sheet of chipboard over my head and looked to see what was inside the tissue. Joy of joys! A sherbet lemon! I slipped the sweet inside my mouth and began to roll it around. I felt my face flush.

A knot of warm lemony pleasurable sensations spread around my palate. I felt little shivers in unexpected zones of my body. My toes begin to tingle. My penis decided to join in the carnival fun, wriggling awake and pressing for a better view. My salivary glands gushed and bubbled merrily. Folly! Sensual distractions! Blurring my – your – awareness of The Barrier. The Barrier trapping me there. There in The Dump. Not the conventional glass wall, not something you come up against like a dull-eyed dim-witted blackbird – SMACK! – hitting a lounge window, no, not like that at all. It was invisible but not tangible. It was a barrier but more like a force field than a wall. Like a rippling, billowing curtain, in fact. You couldn't touch it or stroke it or try to drill a hole in it or smash it with a hammer or blow it open with explosives. These had all been tried, had all failed. Nor did it stay in exactly the same place all the time, as he, The Historian, had proved with the aid of markers. There was no question that it surrounded The Dump, but it was like a sea, subject to tides. There were risings and fallings in its power. There was a theory, a foolish theory... But The Barrier was dangerous if too many people approached it at once. There had been fatalities, serious injuries. The Historian said that rushing it in groups was not advised. When I told Leo he shook his head. My voice made his head ache, he explained. "There is nothing like a good shake of your head to free it of pain and nonsense," he informed me. His clothes were enormous. Far too large for him. Those trousers! He turned a dreadful smile to me. "Insurrection grows irresistibly out of events! The masses make their own history! The art of revolutionary leadership in its most critical moments consists nine-tenths in knowing how to sense the mood of the masses!" Eh? Medium-sized was Leo, with a head-shaped head, upon which he wore a cap of the sort which Lenin used to be fond of. His nose was sharp and upon its bridge perched a pair of grimy granny glasses. A gift, he explained, from his grimy granny. Dot, she insisted on being called at the end, though until her ninety-fourth birthday it had always been Dorothy. His webbed feet? Of no real importance to the tale I have to tell, simply a family quirk. The same can be said of his plump Uncle, Nat, who used to hang around outside the Corn

Exchange in a kangaroo costume until a copper told him to hop off. Of utter irrelevance is his Aunt Martha, who in a thoughtful gesture had the gateway widened for the hearse which she knew would one day need to reverse up her modest suburban driveway. Of little consequence was his Grandmother's parrot, Jolly Boy, trained by a sailor named Baxter amid the stifling heat of Borneo to croak, fluently, "If Democritus were alive now, he should see strange alterations, a new company of counterfeit vizards, whifflers, Cumane asses, maskers, mummers, painted puppets, outsides, fantastic shadows, gulls, monsters, giddy-heads, butterflies!" – after which it would emit a long screech and sham sleep until roused to repeat itself with nuts. "Whifflers?" I enquired, upon first hearing the story of Jolly Boy. "People who whiffle," retorted Leo, flash as a quark. But all this was a long time ago, long before that cold February day when poor Biddle died. I say February and I am reasonably sure though I cannot be absolutely. "February!" ejaculated Leo. "On the 23rd – International Women's Day! – red banners appeared in different parts of the city! 90,000 workers went on strike! Demonstrations, meetings, skirmishes with the police, began in the Vyborg district and spread across the river to the Petersburg side!" Why February? Why so sure? Because of the weather. Intermittent leakages of sunshine lacking in any warmth. On some nights: frost. Most days grey and cold. Misery upon misery. Some days raining from dawn till dusk, others thick with the black promise of storms which never burst. A rum month, all told. But of course I cannot be entirely sure. To all the other insecurities of life in The Dump I must add the worrying loss of my Scenic Views of the West Country Calendar. I relied upon that to get me through the year in a sound state of mind. The satisfactions of ticking off the days and weeks. The one month turned over and the new one begun. The delightful photographs of trawlers at anchor in ports crammed with whitewashed houses and hedgerows brimming with yellow gorse and wild white roses, a robin perching on the nearest twig. The charm of sunlit Lostwithiel merging into The Purple Splendour of Land's End At Dusk. Bodmin Moor under snow. Wave-lashed Tintagel and Merlin's cave. "About one half of the industrial workers of Petrograd were on strike on the 24th of February!" (fragment of Leo's continuing chatter). The day Boodles died I scraped my teeth with a lolly stick and crawled from beneath my sheet of corrugated iron, full of urine and wind. How dimly I recollect the subtle textures of my mood that muggy morning when poor Bangle expired. Another day, indeed! How thickly, falteringly flickers the muddy fluid of my gutter's dribble of consciousness! Another day, another probably February day. Another fucking lousy day. "No, no!" cried Leo. "Not all. For that brave morning the workers made their way in processions to the city centre. More and more people drifted out in the streets. The slogan 'Bread!' had lost its oomph. Now there were cries of 'Down with autocracy!' or 'Down with the war!' Compact masses of workmen sang revolutionary songs!" Shut up. I'm trying to think. Trying to remember. That day. That at-first-sight-same-as-any-other-day. Slept badly, cold, peculiar dreams. A dream about a soup tureen, a dream about a cautious young girl from Penzance, a dream about a sea-green porpoise and a wrapper of scarlet flannel, a dream about Britt Ekland naked in the deserted Chateaux of Nymphenburg, saying (as she says on page one-hundred-and-twenty-one of *Sensual Beauty*), "Personally, I'm all for stretching and the point is to keep going further and further." A dream about a recently married man and his wife's powder-puff, a dream about Sharon Stone, a penis-butter sandwich, the Freudian slop. Bladder full as Loch Morar, rectum bloated as a zeppelin. A plum-sized pile plugging my anus like a champagne cork. A strained expression on my pasty face. Heroic effort involved paralleling attempts on the poles, the top three summits. The explosion rattling windows seventeen miles away. Fingers trembling. A minute or so afterwards the usual agonising dribble. Went back to sleep, if you can call it that. A sort of frozen stupor. "Leo," I said, when I got to know him better. "What exactly *is* whiffling?" He winked. "Knew you'd ask me that sooner or later. Whiffling is –". And then the explosion. "Ah," I said. "I see. Thanks." Then shuffled off in search of the next square meal. "Soldiers in the war hospitals waved from balconies and windows! But the Cossacks kept charging the crowds. Their horses frothed and sweated. People had lost their fear. Crowds surged from one part of the city to another. 'Down with the police!' they bellowed. The mounted police were pelted with stones and lumps of ice. The –". SHUT UP, LEO. Woke about five thirty I should imagine, then again at six. Heard seven chimes an hour or so later. Donggggg... Donggggg... Donggggg... Donggggg... Donggggg... Donggggg... Donggggg... Though "Donggggg" probably creates a misleadingly rich impression of that thin cheap tinny sound. Seven chimes. Without question seven. I counted them one by one. Quite possibly real. Discuss, with reference to omnipotent and impotent narration. Listen! I have heard that there is one place in The Dump from which you can see a church. Allegedly. I have never myself found that place, never seen the old vicarage clock or the alleged spire or the blue, peeling dolphin weathercock which inflamed witnesses have described, merrily adjusting itself to the spasmodic gusts of indecisive wind. "Just shuffling, Leo?" "Shuffling in the archaic sense, Jack. An evasion. A trick. To change the relative positions of. To shift ground. To evade fair questions. Shuffling as whiffling. To wit: prevarication. One who frequently changes his opinion or course to another. The use of evasions. To be fickle or unsteady. From whiffle, a fife or small flute." Sweet Dump! Once, I remember, I excavated a well and sought to escape – bim-bom! – by tunnelling. A deep, deep well. My friends lowered me in a bucket. When I saw it was coming to a finish I shouted at them to stop and they brought the bucket up near level with the end of it. I knew my depth, and I was out of it. Bim-bom. I began to look round, knowing not all the while what I looked for. A warm tunnel enclosing a distant disc of golden light, I suppose. A hole in the wall? Perhaps a chink opening into a mighty cavern. But I could perceive nothing. What made it more difficult was the walls were lined completely with ideology and looked identical. I examined the common sense as closely as I might and took it course by course, til I was afraid of getting giddy. But to little purpose. I called for the working classes but they would not come. My masters could see me and knew no doubt what I was at. "What are you doing?" they cried. "Have you found nothing? Can you see no sunlight?" "No," I called back. "I can see nothing." I feel giddy, feverish. I'm not the man I was. My limbs have turned to jelly. I think I may be a fish. Some sort of eel? "Are you sure you have measured the plummet true?" called a sweet female voice. I heard other voices, harsh and masculine. They talked together. I could not make out what they said for the bim-bom and echo. Then one shouted, "They say you are too high, you must try lower." The bucket began to move lower, slowly. I crouched down in it again, not wishing to look into the dark below. And all the while there rose groanings and moanings from Peruvians, from Paraguayans, as if yammering together that the revolution should be so near. Clear above them I heard the voice of the television, forbidding me to think of such things, telling me of fast women and cars, of empty sandy beaches and capitalism's shine. Such gloss! But I had set foot on this way now and must go through with it. Bim-bom. If you get my drift. Hours later I crawled back to the surface to find everyone gone. I never saw them again. A strange place, The Dump. The stupendous torrs, praecipices and casmas bring amazement, yet courted by delight, that for a time you may seem to have arrested time with admiration; these crested rocks and proud brows of her hills are fann'd with a delicious air: and the delicate breezes that pass through the valleys are a sweet vernal zephyr to refocillate and animate the pasturage; and in winter she hath snow in plenty like a coverlid to keep her herbiage warm. Etcetera. Seven in the morning. Wednesday? So what? The whole fucking cosmos is a load of rubbish, right? A big BANG, right? Next thing there's just leftovers, right? Matter. Who needs it? What does it do? If you ask me: nothing. Bugger antimatter, what I need is a nice cup of tea. Twining's Irish Breakfast, you can't beat it. Almost impossible to get hold of. Have to make a special trip to their shop on the Strand. Afterwards a pint or two at The Edgar Wallace. Dipping my crumpled copy of *Time Regained* into the head. Giving it suck. Sipping and dipping, sipping and dipping. The translation it now turns out was a lot of balls. Went out of print before I'd completed the set. Bastards! Give me a break, play me "Where Are You Tonight?" How I abhor daylight! Hurts my wrinkled eyes. Also I abhor chit-chat. I desire the offspring not of daylight and casual talk. Ah what a blessed relief it is to do without haircuts. That regular ordeal. A blotched creature from twenty-thousand fathoms glaring at me from the bright mirror. The oily attendant with his razors. The stench of spray. The bottles of rose and gold and purple lotions. "Got the day off today, sir? Going out tonight, sir? Going somewhere nice on holiday, sir? See the Arsenal match on Saturday, sir? A shame about the poor Princess, wasn't it sir? Shocking about that bomb, wasn't it, sir?" Cretins. Out there, such garbage! Much better off here. Heard the revised Clause Four? Reminds me of the Treaty of New Echota. Not to mention the Dawes Allotment Act. A dynamic economy! In which the rabid enterprise of the market and the slippery rigour of competition are joined with the fluff of partnership and co-operation to produce profit and yet more profit for the running dogs of capitalism. Casual labour and shit wages! Eh? Where those undertakers, sorry, undertakings essential to the public good are accountable, in a cosmetic sort of way. Bubble bubble bubble. Squeak. Much better off here. No need for grooming here. Grooming, ha! My face a frowzy dirty-coloured red. Give me scruffiness any day. Sloth and dirt. Lolling around. Like today. My day for a lie-in? Or Monday? Or Saturday. The hell with it. Another day. Another fucking lousy day. Turned over, watched the lice shower off me and begin their sport anew on adjacent flesh. Caught a glimpse of myself in a silver hubcap that happened to be nearby. Observed myself phlegmatically. My raw, red, out-of-doors complexion. Hair longer than Lear's. Next moment hair half gone, stinking old age. A clutter of greasy greying strands and decaying shrubs. Teeth no better than the gravestones in the Quaker graveyard by the Nothe fort. Unshaven. Puffy beneath the eyes. A wreck. Fifty? Thirty? Sixty? Hard to say in The Dump. Everyone ages fast. And the smoke and grime and general absence of washing facilities don't help. Today's worldly belongings: a satchel containing a notebook, three apples, a tin of condensed milk, a soiled rag and a lolly stick. A light morning mist spreading across the wastes of The Dump. Lousy meaning mean. Meaning low. Meaning contemptible. Low! You couldn't get much lower. Talk about the Trail of Tears! Sleeping rough in

The Dump. A torn rusty camping mattress underneath my body, my body covered in scabs and sores and feasting creatures with disgusting suction extensions. My body covered by nothing more than a pair of dirty tartan blankets. White trousers brown with dirt, pullover in rags, all the air gone out of my Doc Martens. Anorak mucky. Another day! Time for that first invigorating scratch! Kill one or two of the little blighters. Hopefully. Impossible to make much impression of course. Cripes! Entire battalions of lice burrowing among the shrubs and scabs. Dug in for the winter. No real hope of ever coming across a bottle of toxic lice shampoo, its smell curiously similar to sloe gin. Used to make my hair tingle. In the days when. Another fucking day, yes. But needless to say in spite of that tired expletive no serious hopes of fucking anyone today. Fucking is very rare in The Dump. Because. Because of the smoke and dirt and filth. Because of the wasps, lice, worms. The diseases. The off-putting stench. The lack of romantic situations. The unavailability of sweet, relaxing music. Everyone in the same putrefying, malodorous state. Many of course arrive fresh from Out There. Some in party frocks or even bridal dresses. Some in crisp, nicely ironed cavalry twill. Some in spotless Levis. These new arrivals are inevitably in a condition of shock, anxiety, agitation, fear, melancholy, anguish and perturbation. Copulation is far from their minds. Orgasm is not a pressing need. Those hungriest for sex are those in their first year. They still remember the organised orgasms on Saturday nights and Valentine's Day's desires and slimy embraces under the dripping hairy pier at nightfall and fornication's abandonments in the abandoned fortifications near the pulsing erect lighthouse not to mention fellatio in St. Anton and frenzies amid the Frensham ferns and the pungent moist pines and Acnahannet lust amidst buttock-tickling thistles and sweating tittle-tattle in Seattle and getting the hots at at the Hôtel de Paris and among the loose dunes at drenched Dieppe. The new arrivals naturally do not wish for sexual congress with smeared stinking ragged wretches of indeterminate shape and gender. After the first year, desire ebbs. Something to drink, something to eat, somewhere warm to sleep, those are the three essentials. To keep one's stench down to a reasonable minimum. An absence of toothache. In The Dump, surrounded by detritus and filth, these are the things that really count. Nails, nuts, bolts, trace chains, bits, collars. Sex is just a foolish spasm, a brief sticky inconvenience resulting at worst in diseases and foul-smelling babies. The brown slime. The stunted lives. The consumption, the discarding. A sense of waste amid the vile wastes. Those gripped in the vice of lust invariably resort to fruit and vegetables. The women engage in a brisk trade in carrots and parsnips, the men direct their attentions to marrows. Or pumpkins. There is nothing quite like a fat-bottomed pumpkin to put lead in your pencil. But this lusty phase soon passes. Soon they are as apathetic and listless as the rest of us. Balchin, Lister. Rotting Celia. The others. Too tired, now. Too old. The impulse gone. Total lack of lust in a lacklustre locale. Lacklustre? Not after a fresh shower of aerostat piss. On those days The Dump was as glistening and brown as Mozart's last dying vomit. Repeat myself? Of course I bloody well do! Guzzle and dribble. Whizzpoppers. Reminds me of the day I encountered the sign to Clinton. Thanks. I have it! By that day I had long since given up any wish to plug my discoloured but still precious penis into a slimy dangerous socket located inside a complete stranger who harboured unknown thoughts. It did not take long to get there. Inside Clinton was an odour of human faeces, pungent and raw, very reminiscent of the open drains of St. Anton-am-Arlberg. There was a strange echoing, as if Clinton was a soot-black railway arch and I was huddled underneath, hearing a dull and empty echo leadenly bouncing to and fro on the dirty brickwork. It was on the evening of the second day that I encountered an unidentifiable piece of brown fruit coated in a shimmer of off-white maggots. Beyond it lay the yellow-green pools of urine, rainbow-shimmery pools of enticing toxicity, and on the shore a heap of rags, a silver hypodermic. Feverish and fretful I floundered around Clinton, teetering and grimacing as I staggered past the wall of crazy mirrors. I began to run my fingers over the keyboard. Soon it was Tuesday. I had spotted a piano earlier in the day. I can't remember exactly what I played. Fragments here and there mixed in with a lot of improvisation. The transitions as abrupt as

Washington State's, in your remembered days there. Clinton's smile is a strange, desolate region, dung-brown, with a painful glare. The insincerity reminded me of an egg yolk cultured with salmonella, both homely and poisonous. I was reminded of the folk who ring your doorbell and say, "Hi!" and tell you their first name, which is always Mike ("Hi! I'm Mike!"), and then ask if you are the houseowner ("Hi! I'm Mike! Are you the houseowner?") and then when you say "No" the expectant eyes grow dull, the smile ebbs, the shoes retreat back to the street. In time, as ever, I left that region of terrible echoes. The first thing to be done was to see to my pistol. You will perhaps notice that I had lied, earlier. I was born in a short street that opened off a square. Inside the rectangle (for how many squares are square?) there stood a public urinal, a statue of a famous man named Alexandre-Auguste Ledru-Rollin, two sandstone benches, and twenty-four lime trees. As a boy I would cross the square dizzy and nauseous at the thought of Clinton's vast vistas of emptiness. Such hollowness. Bim-bom! When I at last emerged my face mask was coated in shining amber filth. Daylight washed over me. I bellowed with a strange ardour, with an avidity rarely seen in these days of wind and drivel. "Long live the glorious October revolution!" is one interpetation, highly plausible if you ask me. It was then that I became aware that someone had entered the room. A nurse? The Prime Minister? "I hope you don't mind me making these sounds. There didn't seem to be anybody about." "Not in the least," said the Prime Minister. "It's a relief to hear something different from this appalling situation we're in." "It is true then? About Europe I mean?" I ask you! Requesting the truth from that clammy pobble! That glossy mucilaginous pillar of blab and slither! Expecting an honest answer from that truckling, bobbing, pliant, unctuous, windy, creeping Jesus! A man whose fixed smirk showed him to be oblivious to Hegel's contention that only one body of mutually coherent propositions is possible. Ignorant equally was he of Dewey's argument that empiricists use propositions as the means of inquiring into things and events which are the materials and objects of inquiry, not to mention the consonance between Reichenbach's probability theory and the argument that things are a metaphysical delusion and that the truth of basic propositions depends upon their relation to some occurrence, and that the truth of other propositions depends upon their syntactical relations to basic propositions. As a boy I would cross the square to get fresh bread from the baker's and when I had glanced at the sky and all twenty-four trees, to make sure that they had neither multiplied nor disappeared, I would study the surface of the square. Extraordinary, the things that I found through that habit. A woman's handkerchief; a button-hook; a box of mysterious medicine in the shape of globular, transparent pills; a bill with an excessive discount for cash payment made out by my own father; and, once, an illegal incitement to revolution, which cried through the medium of smudged printing: "Citizens Unite!" The next day I took my first, faltering steps in the direction of the vanished republic. For lack of even the most essential data, I am able to say little about the People's Socialist Republic of Nambuangongo, other than that it was established around February 1961 in the Dembos forests in north-western Nambuangongo (between the rivers Loge and Lang) in the immediate wake of the 1961 rising in Luanda. Changing direction, I came across a sack of old telegrams. BAFFLED AND HURT BY YOUR SILENCE STOP PLEASE GET IN TOUCH STOP EELS STOP TELL ERICA NOT TO WORRY STOP CHARLES STOP PLEASE PHONE REGARDING DORCAS STOP URGENT STOP VICKY STOP WHATEVER HAPPENED TO DORCAS STOP GEORGE STOP AM GOING TO ALEPPO STOP DO NOT TRY AND CONTACT ME STOP ALICE STOP Eels? Dorcas? Sounds like a bloody sitcom. Sitcom? So far I have said nothing about the light entertainment side of things here in The Dump. Sometimes it is possible to watch situation comedies. Sometimes even the news. Frequently alas reception is only achieved in time for the pathos of the final item, after which, all too frequently, the image dissolves into a moment's abstract expressionist masterpiece, all barbs and colliding coils, white incandescent sparklings, after which, invariably, the screen goes dead. The final item! Designed to cheer up the viewer up after those gabbling ministers and agitated witnesses and survivors and the fires and crashes and murders and shoot-outs and assaults and the dense dark smoke the colour of mushroom soup billowing prettily upward amid the villages of a sunlit landscape faraway. How, in time, they blur together. Stranded whales and royal tours and oily sea-birds and dogs and princes, the courtiers wagging their tails, the prune-faced sour-eyed monarch – Ickpling Gloffthrobb Squutserumm blhiop Mlashnalt Zwin tnodbalkguffh Slhiophad Gurdlubb Asht! – resting her tons of blubber upon her massive stomach and vast, elongated arse. The anchor-man coated in deference, everything bright and sleek and shining with a rainbow-hued slime, the putrefaction barely visible, the stench not to be nosed. And not just news! In The Dump the opportunity does not often arise to go to the movies for there are no cinemas. In my wanderings I have never encountered a projectionist (which does not mean to say that they don't exist). I have never come across discarded screens or rusting projectors. Nevertheless it is occasionally possible to take in a good film. This is all thanks to the unstinting endeavours of one or two film-crazed individuals and technological whizzkids who have made it their business to forage for old video recorders, lengths of flex and abandoned batteries. Once in a blue moon the batteries function and the elaborate wiring works and you get the chance to watch a good film – always provided you have the price of admission. Prices vary. Sometimes a ticket of admission to a video-show ditch costs (say) a Valium tablet, two cans of beer, twenty bars of soap, two tins of talcum powder, four toilet rolls (soft tissue) or something which the admissions man regards as being of equivalent value. Complete sets of the works of Scott or Dickens are not welcome, but deals can often be thrashed out involving bars of chocolate, boiled sweets or grotesque sexual favours. The choice of films on offer is very limited, and usually involves those which people have thrown out as being either boring or completely unwatchable. But oddly enough these are just the kinds of film which people in The Dump seem to enjoy. Firm favourites are *The War Game*, *Les Jeux Interdits* and *Stalker*. Living off the thin of the land has its compensations, eh? Sossing in an easy chair, mildewed and blotched. As for the chair! But things could be worse, eh? Better off am I than the six million child workers of Pakistan who work in carpet factories, brick-making plants, on farms and as servants. I'm better off than Iqbal Masih who was sold into slavery aged four and who spent the next six years chained to a carpet-weaving loom tying tiny knots between 4 am and 4 pm each day and who was shot dead at the age of twelve in the village of Muritke twenty miles from Lahore on Sunday 23 April 1995. I'm better off than the young women workers in New Vietnam's Export Processing Zones who work a twelve-hour day at a basic rate of £12 a month. Not to mention the workers in the garment and micro-electronics factories of Shenzhen who work twelve to fifteen-hour shifts, live in damp dormitories and have one of the highest rates of industrial accidents anywhere in the world. I'm better off than factory workers contaminated by toxic dioxins as a consequence of exposure to chlorine-based products burned in incinerators who suffer from weakened immune systems and reduced testosterone levels. I may be covered in scabs and infested with lice and worms but at least I'm alive! No nine to five grind for yours truly, no sir! If I want a lie in, I have a lie in, no matter what I'm lying in. Shit! Things could be a lot worse, eh? I might, after all, have been part of the population of Tokyo's shitamachi a little after midnight on the morning of 10 March 1945 when 334 B-29 Superfortresses began dropping 1,539 tons of incendiary bombs during a three-hour bombardment in which 270,000 buildings and 15.8 square miles were razed and people burned bubbling and popping and hissing alive in their homes, or choking coughing hysterical gasping were overcome by fumes, or were boiled bubblingly alive as they leaped into seething bubbling boiling canals. Better off (much better off) than people in Somalia and Egypt etc. (Long list here, eh?) Makes yer proud, considering. Da da da da da da da, da da da da da da, da da da da da da da da dumb dumb dumb dumb dumb dumb. Yush! Thoil-oil-ways-bin-un-un-gland-woil-thuz-a-cunt-tree-loin, wireover-thuz-a-cut-age-smell, beshite-a-toxic-foiled. Da da. February 27. Slept badly in the afternoon. Everything is changed. O I ha'e Silence left, yes. Farewel. At present all I can write would be but the history of my miserable feelings. Thus I was tossed and so perplexed, especially at some times, that I could not tell what to do. I saw myself in a forlorn and sad condition; and would also often, with lifting up of heart, sing that of the fifty-first Psalm, O Lord, consider my distress; for as yet I knew not where I was. Possibly in Komsomolsky, shovel in hand. Banished. Learning how to eke out my miserable days. A good word, eke. Ee as in knee. Eke as in creak. And me on my knees, creaking in every joint. Tormented by arthritis, red hot needles stabbing into my phalanges and ginglymoids. A glowing poker thrust up my tight, squirming arse. My head beginning to crack with aches. As if some preposterous metaphysical entity was zooming in. Taking the mick out of the Kalmyks. Making me sweat for a lifetime of unspeakable pleasures. Punishing me for my dreams. Mocking my mockery of a life. Pissing colourfully on the tattered sallow descendants of the Golden Horde. Demoralising yours truly as he tends as best he can his squalid vegetable plot beside a ramshackle hut. Withered, curling cabbages going brown. Shrivelled carrots. Oozing sour sweetcorn looking like a nose covered in scabs. Sand getting everywhere. Into my eyes, my mouth, my dripping nostrils. Into my curdled carrot soup. Into my rickety hut. My hut? A labour of love. Old rotting fenceposts with knuckles of wire deftly intertwined with corrugated sheeting, enticingly rustpatched with blotches oddly reminiscent of the crumbling stacks east of Ballard Downs. The wind blew it down. The structure sank into the sand. Perhaps it never existed. Just one of those ditch-dreams you sometimes get. A hut! A nice cosy hut! Instead of this open-air filth, this ditch half full of plastic containers and rat droppings and scraps of oily blairspeeches. For several days, remembering my bright ditch-dream, I was greatly assaulted and perplexed, and was often ready to sink where I went, with faintness in my mind. But one day, after I had been so many weeks cast down therewith, as I was now quite giving up the ghost of all my hopes of ever attaining life, this sentence fell with weight upon my spirit, *All that is solid melts into air, all that is holy is profaned.* "Chin up," I said to myself. "Things could be worse. At least you were never a motorist." Motorists find life in The Dump particularly hard. It is difficult to say which is worst – separation from their car or the loss of

65

mobility. Poor wretches. Some sit for days in solitary, broken front passenger seats, reprising commercials. They reach through the gaps in their shredded shell suits, listlessly scratching the leaking sores around their genitals while their rotting minds project sun-drenched Z-bends where dark-haired sun-glassed women loiter by the flanks of gleaming saloons, moist with desire, skirts pushed up against their strong bronzed thighs, waiting to be pleasured by a vacuum unit fixing screw as white foam explodes against those backdrop Mediterranean rocks beyond the glowing band of pure untarnished sand. Some hum old Clapton tunes redolent of speed and throbbing stereo systems, the gusts of empty motorways at dawn, the harsh manly screech of rubber marking heroic getaways on the tarmac. Some devote their remaining days to reconstructing their heart's delight, often starving to death before completion. They trade wizened but serviceable carrots for crankshaft sprockets, swop reasonable potatoes for pistons and big-end bearing caps. I remember one, a mechanic, a greasy, gruesome, blair-eyed, overalled, nixonish sort of man, of average torso, who constructed a car from scratch, obtaining engine support bolts, camshaft retainer plate and clutch driveshaft screw by dint of theft and buggery. Luminous with stupid delight was his dripping rodent's face as he twisted the pipe-cleaner and got it going. So happy was this wretch that he drank an entire bottle of meths to celebrate. Roaring off at speed, he collided seconds later with a traffic island (which, as he pointed out, dying, hadn't been there the day before). The vehicle erupted like a car-bomb and he was, I'm delighted to say, hideously burned. He died, surrounded by an excited crowd, in agony. Sheets of white, dripping skin hung from him like champagne-splashed flags. But most never get that far. Most sit alone, clutching rootless steering wheels, blubbering. For a week or so they find consolation with other sufferers and exchange long stories of hold-ups on the M5 and short-cuts through Surrey and which lane to get into when entering the Hanger Lane gyratory system and the time they had to wait two hours for the AA and how they slithered on Snake Pass in the snow and the time they had to wait three hours on the A606 because of the cones and the road menders weren't even working, just drinking tea, and how best to avoid the jams in Brent. And then they die, holding their ignition keys with personalized key ring. Key rings portraying their initials in upper-case gold, or miniatures of their favourite Porsche, or of their blonde girlfriends. The lower-middle classes die with a puzzled frown, clutching hub caps or number plates which contain their initials or their date of birth. In The Dump there is simply nowhere to drive a car, and this, in their eyes, is a nightmare greater than death, which is everywhere. You might manage to accelerate ten metres past the heap of sacks on your left but beyond that, you can be certain, lies rough, impenetrable ground, broken glass, a patch of burning rubbish gushing fierce flames and thick dense black choking smoke, a ditch, a pool of oil, a toxic residue, a bubble of explosive gas just waiting for some prick to pierce its flimsy membrane. Death is everywhere in The Dump, which is why there is nothing like coming across a good obituaries page to perk you up. The younger or more famous the better. Serve the bastards right. The unexpected death of Labour MP John McSmug has come as a great shock to our galaxy. Three purple-skinned paranoid humanoids on Jupiter were seen openly weeping, and as a mark of respect McSmug's favourite piece of music – Karlheinz Krzcecebit's Obtuse Variations in F Minor for Whistle and Anus – are to be broadcast unceasingly for the next seventeen years in all telephone booths on the asteroid belt. John McSmug died yesterday while attempting simultaneously to devour a mushroom omelette, a buttered croissant, two slices of toast and marmalade, a bacon butty, a crumpet topped with greengage jam and a bowl of peaches and cream while drinking a half pint of whisky. McSmug was heard to say to his cleaning woman, "I feel I'm getting bigger," when, without warning, he exploded. All the windows in his luxury penthouse apartment were blown out as lumps of McSmug showered down on passers-by. McSmug came from a humble bourgeois Scottish background. After several years at Edinburgh University, where he is still vividly remembered as "even in those days an unctuous, oily, ambitious little creep", he became a barrister, specialising in defending companies from charges of negligence made against them by limbless or poisoned workers. His retort to one claimant – "You say you were poisoned by toxic dust and malodorous chemicals, but I say to you it is your mind that is poisoned – poisoned by left-wing troublemakers and a lot of silly speculation about pollution put about by lunatic environmentalists" – is fondly remembered even today by the legal establishment. And. And the death has been announced of Gavin Blore, General Secretary of the Union of Boltmakers and Flex-worglers. Widely tipped as a future TUC leader, Mr Blore had been ill for some time from regressive softening of the spine. Gavin Blore joined the U.B.F.W. when he was fourteen, as a tea-boy. His ingratiating manner, mental vacuum, hatred of strikes and enthusiasm for laying out the papers at committee meetings soon brought him to the attention of his superiors, and by the age of eighteen he was a full-time official, with special responsibility for demoralising members engaged in local disputes. His attitude to filing-cabinet systems earned him widespread respect in the Labour movement. And. And the death has been announced of Sir Nicholas Swill. Swill will always be remembered as of one the most colourful personalities the House of Commons has yet thrown up – a glistening mass of turd browns dappled with streaks of chocolate and attractive bright splashes of red, redolent of the bowel cancer which finally killed this turbid fascist. He will be fondly remembered by his many friends in journalism, television and politics. Yup, there's nothing like an obituary to cheer up yours truly. And quite frankly those of us who inhabit The Dump need all the cheering up we can get. Newspapers are a real boon in such circumstances. Once, I remember, I encountered a newcomer, a tattooed man in rags. He was holding up a home-made placard that read ANUS. At first I admired his flexible attitude to market realities. Having nothing to sell other than his body he was prepared to rent out any orifice that might earn him a few pennies from a passing sodomite. Having long since given up orgasms I naturally had no interest in responding to his enterprise. To my surprise and dismay he no sooner saw me than he bounded towards me across the waste. "I'm not gay," I snapped irritably as he grunted and pawed at me. It took some time to discover that he was in fact a vigorous young working-class masturbator in a state of considerable nervous agitation at having been separated from his favourite daily newspaper. Only semi-literate, he was also prone to dyslexia, hence his misleading placard. I reversed the sign and wrote on the back what it was he was seeking: A SUN. This is The Barbarians' favourite newspaper, named after a sphere of hydrogen and helium gas. I told the youth that I had never yet come across a copy in The Dump. Besides, I cautioned him, looking at it for long periods can seriously damage your eyesight. "You may even go blind!" He shook his head, as if to say: "What rot!" Thanking me for correcting his placard, he scurried away, saying he had an appointment to keep. The Dump, The Dump. A queer place. Eight hundred square miles of garbage. At the very least. A tip, literally. Prone to sudden subsidence. Heap upon heap of piled rubbish. Place of sludge and stains, landscape of dregs and draff and sweepings. Ah, the gleam of feculence and mildew! One day Jesus tapped me on the shoulder, said, "John, why are you resisting me?" I said, "I'm not called John. What's more, to be brutally honest, do you know how bad you smell? You smell about two thousand years old. And the stuff that's clinging to your sandals. As for that prayer of yours. I always had this image of God as a fat, red-faced landowner who put up PRIVATE KEEP OUT notices all round his estate, and who hated trespassers." Jesus shook his head. "The meek shall inherit the earth," he said. I said: "Yeah, but only if they grasp their power as workers within the capitalist system, and benefit from the presence of a revolutionary socialist party with substantial roots in the class able to help them understand the reformism of the trades-union leadership and to see that the structures of the capitalist system – parliament, the police, the army, the judiciary – cannot be reformed but must be smashed and replaced by a workers' state based upon councils of workers' delegates and a workers' militia." Jesus looked a bit perplexed. He was silent for a while. Then he brightened. From under his dirty robe he produced a folding table, some Sainsbury's croissants, a packet of rainbow trout and some cups of water. He proceeded to perform some very impressive conjuring tricks. "Hey, not bad," I said, munching a grilled trout sandwich and sipping a very agreeable glass of full-bodied red wine which I could have sworn was made from Fer Servadou grapes. Afterwards I clubbed him over the head with the empty, rigged up a rough cross and crucified the bastard. It was at this point that I discovered Jesus had no sense of humour. The things he said to me! A couple of days later someone made off with the corpse, almost certainly to recycle it for kebabs and burgers. Time passed, passes. Night, sleep, piss. Another day! I have some unfinished business in Tepl, too bad. The emerald mould, the billowing fungus. The cesspools stinking under a rancid sun! A plain tangled with remnants, remainders, rumps and stumps, scrag-ends and dog-ends, stubs and bones. Wreckage! Débris! Place of ruins. Learn to make shift with the leftovers. One morning I encountered a tall, thin-faced leather-jacketed male biped identical, almost, to M in *L'Année dernière à Marienbad*. He was hand in hand with a denim-jacketed female who greatly resembled the silent-movie star Marie Prevost (who, after dying, was eaten by her dachshund). We passed in silence. Ah, what a touching sight is love and friendship! I am on my way to the Dianahof, to think about her while staring at my butter dish. Drink up that cracked cup of watery sediment, whore! Bathe amid scum, old friend. Feast on peelings, comrades! This is the zone for those whose services have not been retained by the company! Dump of the expired, the unconsumed, the depleted. Ravel out weaved-up follies. The Dump, The Dump. A good three Glonglungs in length if you ask me. Here you are truly useless, truly superfluous, truly inadequate and unemployable. Place of muck and dross! I fall upon the thorns of life. I seep! I ooze and drip. I vent stenches. What's more I've had a dicky ankle for weeks. But don't you worry about me. You go on enjoying yourself, out there beyond The Great Barrier. After all, there's heaps of vitamins in orange peel and potato peel and carrot peel and turnip peel. I can pretend I'm at the Schloss Balmoral & Osborne. I can suck wood when times get tough. And what's wrong with rags? I dress like everyone else, in scraps. Old clothes, cast-offs. Bits of carpet. A nice pair of trousers with the name Len-something daubed at the back with a marker pen. Dump of functionless folk, purposeless people, pointless ambitions, unworkable dreams, effort-wasting aspiration. That Russian I once met. Alexander. Toiling on his own to raise a cathedral. A structure made out of rubbish, including dark red plastic trays from a bakery. The spire reminiscent of a witch's hat. Seven days he toiled, and in the evening of the seventh the entire structure collapsed. A fascinating figure was Alexander, with his paunch and his Nietzsche moustache. One morning he just wasn't there. This often happens. Come and go. Erasures and deletions. Thin spectral figures. An Irishman clutching a lengthy, much-annotated recipe for Mulligan Stew. Dump of cast-offs and time-yellowed offprints. A torn package with half a dozen bright Italian stamps addressed to Professor Binns. Wasn't he in *Loch Ness*? Starring Lemuel Gulliver and Constance Chatterley? It's a small world, eh? Dump of poor Joe Beaumont, of whom more later, perhaps. Perhaps not. Dump of broken videos and chucked-out paperbacks and nonreturnable bottles and all that is superfluous, expendable, unneeded, unwanted. Things and people once fit as a fiddle, now fit for nothing. Built-in obsolescence, the very marrow of every gleaming product. And people. You give the best years of your life for the company, for the economy, for England – and then? Dumped. Just like that. Made redundant. Globalism. Can't be helped, say those fuckers rolling in dosh. Barristers, politicians, media creeps. Glossy and sleek. Whereas we here are shabby and blotched. Broken down, outmoded, bootless. Prone to giddiness, given to tottering. No cheap cracks s'il vous plait. Here we are not worth the paper we're written on, eh? Worthless as Argentinian bonds, polluted as an English river, filthy as a saddle of British beef. Here there is nothing to write home about. Here, at best, all you can hope for is an epic of bits and pieces, of odds and ends, of ended odds and odd ends. But mustn't grumble, eh? No matter how bad things are in The Dump at least I'm better off than the six million child workers of Pakistan, eh? Mustn't grumble. Some mornings Lady Luck smiles. You step past a fly-encrusted rib-cage, jump a puddle of rainbow-hued oil and spot, lying on a pink scrap of *The Financial Times*, not yet pierced by wasps or worms, an apple. An honest English apple! A September's Bramley, April-fresh thanks to a stiff dose of carbon dioxide and nitrogen gas in the silo in which it has been stored, a homely metallic structure with a bracing whiff of this and of that. Glory be to God for modified atmosphere storage! Glory be to God for waxed cucumbers! Glory be to God for Tecnazene to spray upon potatoes inhibiting sprouting! Glory be to God for fungicides W230-233 to make our citrus fruits and bananas wholesome as the creator intended! Glory be to God for salmon dye and gas-flushed fish! Glory be to God for gas-ripened apricots! Glory be to God for the market, for Lo! did not the first bourgeois economist Adam Smith say e'en in the glorious eighteenth century, "It is in the nature of every man to trick, fart and get laid." Let us spray, let us spray, let us ask no questions. Sleep now, your maggoty narrator insists upon it. For every word hath its marrow in the English tongue for order and for delight. Tea anyone? Tea and sleep and sweet dreams and another night gone by. Next another day, another fucking day. Correction. Another fuckless day. Those were the days, eh? The good old days. When I was still interested. When I'd think: fucking on a day like today? Fat chance! Haven't met a soul for weeks, let alone a woman, a nice ripe amenable juicy woman with a sense of humour and an easy-going fuck-me attitude to life. The women I've met in The Dump aren't interested in sex. Gone off it. Or never went in for it in the first place. Won't do it for fear of disease. Pregnancy. Worms. Loyalty To Another. Crabs. Lice. Piddling objections like that. Makes a man sick. "More interested in other things", as one of them said to me. Forget her name. Trish? Other things! I ask you! More interested in giving gentle suck to a banana, sipping the last drops of yellow-brown mulch. Twisted. Pathetic. Totally uninterested in eight inches of throbbing penis. (Well alright, five and a half inches.) (Oh very well, four inches, and not a centimetre less.) Unbelievable. What's gone wrong with the world? I've still got my looks, haven't I? I'm still young, aren't I? I still stiffen, don't I? It's not as if they are anything to write home about. Mucky Mary. Louse-encrusted Lil. Dirty Diana. Filthy Felicity. Said what made me attractive was my habit of incessantly cleaning the nails of one hand with the nails of the other. And, when seated, rubbing the sole of my long right foot up my left shin, disseminating a grave-like odour. As for Sarah. Safe sex with her was nothing to write home about. She rigged up a tape of "Moonlight Becomes You" and sucked on a beet to get me going. A parsnip up the rectum, I ask you! Fucking confabulators, all of them. Prefer versification to the real thing. A perverted enthusiasm for prosody. Rub your crotch and think of Walthamstow. Walking up the High Street, two carrier bags of groceries in each hand. The signs of the stallholders. CHEDDER CHEESE. ANTI-FREZZ. Each stall blaring the same song on the transistor radios. The longest street market in Europe, fucking feels like it, how many times have I trudged it, hundreds, thousands, know every fucking inch of it, in rain, in snow, in sleet, in hail, in tropical heat, most of them on grey dull featureless days. *Watch me fucking jogglies!* screamed the stallholder obscurely as I brushed his bottoms with my bike. Ah, memory! The old days, the days before The Dump. You get back there to that littered street via an electrical impulse. Cool. Propagated is it down the axon conveying a message to the next cell. One nerve cell excites, another inhibits. Different cells releasing different chemical substances. That's neurotransmitters to you, mate. Affecting the next cell. The miry message is transmitted across the synapse by about forty different neurotransmitters. Did you know that different cells release different neurotransmitters? Of course you bleedin' didn't. And different neurotransmitters predominate in different parts of the brain. How can I put it? A black hole leading straight to an old April. Neil Young singing "Heart of Gold". The years, the changes, all before The Dump. Oh shut it, SHUT IT! When I doe think back I doe know how verrie luckie I bee ande wythe soe muche toe bee thankful for how toe rite and figger. Eh? Your words no more clear, can hardly swim. I alternate between spells of fatigue and indifference. Eh? Once, I remember, I took a cabbage into town to buy some cloisters. Once I dreamed of putting on a double-breasted reefer jacket, white nankeen sailors' trousers and black leather boots and setting sail for Lerici. The years passed. I favoured the exercises of Professor Müller. I starved, dreaming of spicy sausages the size of an elephant's prick. I craved a pint of iced lager in Alexandria – or the Rose & Crown. The TV was babbling. "War is not a humane activity," said General Johnson. "The United States was in the war to win." Deranged. You know I'd give anything to get out of this place, even if it was only for a few days. Just to do the ordinary things again – use a telephone, walk in a dogshit-smeared park, puke on a carpet, fall downstairs, piss in a phone box, spend money, and have to make a decision. Excreting, accreting. Accreting memories, experiences. Accretion amid the castoffs, paradox, bah! Where are they, the great hostesses of the ilk of Sibyl Colefax and Emerald Cunard? Beautiful things. The blue teapot. The gold eggcup. The fish knives. And all of them royal. The royal insignia. The regimental drums. Cretinous. Having lost all their faculties they sat motionless in their various chairs, some looked at television with their eyes closed. Me too. My eyes, my ears are going, everything is going. My legs are going. My arms are going. Quick! A brisk narrative transition. She had broken her hip but was still full of sparkle. Ah, the old days. We never stopped dancing. I doted on her, you know. Eh? Wanted: more Personality and Decision Making. Give me my boots, I say! Eh? Wanted: more analysis of the structure of words (morphology), more sounds of a given language (phonology), more systems of versification (prosody). Cup of tea? What's this? A headline? Bliss! *TUBERCULOSIS THREATENS THIRD OF WORLD'S PEOPLE, W.H.O. WARNS. Tuberculosis, once considered a vanquished Victorian disease, is spreading rapidly throughout the world because of failure to use low-cost drugs which can cure it, the World Health Organisation said yesterday. The disease will kill at least 30 million people over the next decade, and could infect more than a third of the world's population – some 2 billion people – the WHO warns in a report published in New York.* I cheered vigorously. In my imagination. In real life (joke!) I emitted one or two croaks, like a punctured frog. The newspaper was old and sodden. When I tugged at the page it ripped silently away. The light was bad. I screwed up my eyes, tried to make out a day, a month, a year. Nineteen-ninety-five already! Jesus, three years out at least! I'd been convinced it was still nineteen-ninety-two. But now I knew it was nineteen-ninety-five or maybe even later. Nineteen-ninety-six, or even seven. Had we reached the new millennium yet? I did not think so. I had seen no fireworks. I was reasonably convinced it was not yet the next century. Stretched out on a sodden roll of carpeting I idly fingered the encompassing muck. A worm. An empty two litre plastic lemonade bottle. A few tabloid newspapers from the early eighties. Some recent broadsheets. I sprang to my feet and ran across to Bodge. "Marvellous news, Bodge! Israeli planes have bombed the village of Nabatiyet, killing a mother, her seven children (one a four-day old girl) and two teenage relatives! That will teach 'em to go on soaking up the Lebanese sun and ignoring our plight here in The Dump, eh? And listen to this! Four gunmen screaming 'God is great' machine-gunned a coachload of elderly Greek tourists, killing seventeen! They are dead and we are alive! How sweet the scent of death is. How delightful to know that The Barbarians are keeping up the good work, zapping fellow Barbarians without cease! Hurrah! More wars please! More terrorist atrocities! And *do* keep driving that car as much as possible, eh? Last year's road casualty statistics were phenomenal! This year's promise to be even better. So keep that accelerator pedal pressed down hard, my friend. More air bags, more recklessness! Things are distinctly getting amusing out there! Thirty million to die in the next ten years!" Bodge beamed. He was draining a few inky drops from the stagnant base of a dirty Martini bottle. "Good ol' Henri Paul!" he slurred. "Give us something to talk about, eh? October the First is Too Late!" He burbled and burped. I could see I'd cheered Bodge up no end. He was a tall good-natured youth, his father born in Penge. "A third of the world's population infected, did you say?" He grinned. Molatuendalaas! "That's what this report says, yes. Here, see for yourself." "Bloody marvellous," grinned Bodge. "Bloody, bloody marvellous." He departed in high spirits, vaulting over a nearby oil drum in a manner which reminded me of scenes from *The Wooden Horse*. Alas, dietary deficiencies and high-altitude pulmonary edema had sapped poor Bodge's strength. His scrotum slammed into the rim of the drum and he screamed in agony. Picking up an adjacent pomegranate, spitting out pips and patches of musty-tasting mildew, I watched with interest as Bodge fell to the ground in slow motion and made writhing motions. "Fuck! Shit! Buggabuggabuggabuggabugga!" he said, sounding like a fashionable Scottish novelist when at last able to emit language. I made the most of the situation. Kicking Bodge in the face, I ran off with his radio. Christ! Hear that! Thought For The Day! Remnants of the old life. Everyone had a Thought For The Day. Mostly it was: Survive At All Costs! Or: Must Get More Food Today! Or: It's bram an gathe. Or: Christ I'd Give Anything For A Cool Glass Of Lager! Or: I Wonder If Christine Would Let Me Fuck Her For This Tin Of Peaches? Moi, j'y pense tous les soirs. Alors, attention Emily! Regarde-moi dans les yeux. Allez! Little crotchets and curves of her own (and what curves!). Fucked and lost, squeezed out and lost. Lost for words. The sadness, the waste. The shame. Precious time spilled on idle conversation. Consuming alcohol. Sweaty satisfying sex. Time which might have been better spent – spent! – discussing or at any rate accumulating information about Ionian Speculation or Descartes' Epistemology or Spinoza's Ethics or Locke's Theory of Knowledge or Berkeley's Idealism or Hegel's Philosophy of History or Marx's Historical Materialism or Kierkegaard's Christian Existentialism or what to do if you tear your thoracic cartilage or Weber's Historical Sociology or the ins and outs of Nietzsche's Perspectivism or James's Pragmatism or Habermas' Critical Theory or coded references to masturbation in the diaries of Matthew Arnold or Kuhn's Paradigm or Quine's Ontological Relativism or Byron's letter to John Cam Hobhouse of October 12, 1821, or Rorty's Neo-Pragmatism, enough to drive anyone to drink. Or even something practical and likely to be of use in the late capitalist era. The psychology of selling. Telephone power. The secrets of closing the sale. How to win customers and keep them for life. How to power-pack your days. Time and stress management. How to unleash your imagination and clear away those pesky idea traps that hold other people back. How to win the game when you are playing in someone else's ballpark. Discover the secrets of leadership. Reverse the ageing process with special herbs and a top-secret recipe handed down by monks. Put pep into middle-age with melatonin supplements.

Obtain Australian citizenship and stay on top when your world turns upside down. Use the latest techniques to overcome your fear of alien abduction. Lose weight at Dachau. Experts help you to apply the latest communication techniques in dealing with young goats. World famous thinker V. I. Lenin reveals the secrets of building up a successful organisation and how to cope with difficult people. Let image expert Ronald Reagan help YOU to communicate confidently and clearly. *In Tough Times Tough People Stick It Out*: Nobel Prize Winning Author Slim Y. Bucker shows how to cope with setbacks, identify threats and create new opportunities. What's that? Give you more data? More of that monstrous mass that accrues from the moment-by-moment of a life? Friends and oneself by now somewhat tired and elderly. Elderly and forgetful. Forgetful and irritable. Ha – ha! Keep time! Prone, alas, to exaggerate. To suppress. Full of gorgeous inventions and fib. Anything to sharpen the story. Lewdness, even. Filth! Living here amid cardboard boxes, treasures. A film of dust over everything. Old snapshots. Faded Polaroid snaps of cunt and cock. Of rumps and squelch. My eyesight, my digestion, my joie de vivre, all quite gone. Jack-of-the-clock. The end is in sight. Ho there! Fetch me my binoculars! My binoculars? One day I came across a pair of in The Dump. It was a crisp February day and I'd spent a not very rewarding morning rummaging through a heap of commercial refuse – rusting filing cabinets, faded swivel chairs, rolls of tatty mildewed carpet. So far the best thing I'd come across was a Mickey Mouse pencil sharpener and a miniature bottle of gin which had fallen down the back of somebody's filing cabinet drawer. I spent a long time sniffing the gin before I drank it. I even splashed a drop on my skin to see if it was really acid. You can never be too careful in The Dump. There's nothing The Malevolents like more than finding empty bottles and filling them up with unpleasant or even downright dangerous liquids. I've known newcomers to The Dump whoop with joy at the sight of a golden bottle of fifteen-year-old Laphroaig, unscrew the cap, take a deep gulp and – "Aaaaaaaaaaaaaaagh! Yuuuuuuuuuugh!" Puke! You guessed. Not whisky at all but malt urine. Once I came across a smartly dressed city type with a briefcase and a recent copy of *The Times* at his side. He was slumped in a ditch, his back against the muddy side, his pinstriped legs splayed out, stiff as corrugated iron. Dead. About twelve hours dead, at a rough guess (you can learn a lot about rigor mortis in The Dump if you make the effort, and believe me it sets in a lot quicker than most people realise). City Type was holding in his right hand a bottle of gin. The label showed a beefeater and the Tower of London, but whatever was in that bottle wasn't the genuine article at all. A Malevolent had filled the bottle with hydrochloric acid or similar. Whatever it was had snuffed out City Type on the spot. His lips were drawn back in a terrible snarl, his teeth bared like a tetanus sufferer. His eyes were screwed up and glaring. Dead as a door-knocker. So when I saw the gin miniature I didn't allow my emotions to run away with me. First of all I checked for booby traps (sometimes The Malevolents attach trip wires to interesting-looking things such as booze, objets d'art, tempting packing-cases). I've seen people snatch at something like a bottle of port, next thing it blows up in their face, or a precariously poised car chassis comes crashing down on them. *USEFUL TIPS 1. Never allow your emotions to run away with you. You never know where they may lead you. 2. Before picking up an interesting object, whether it is a book, a bottle of booze or an unmildewed cushion, examine it carefully for wires, string and black cotton. 3. Avoid rummaging for food or souvenirs in comfy-looking ditches which have old cardboard boxes, agricultural machinery or wrecked cars piled at the edges. It may be a trap.* As it happens, I was in luck. There were no wires or other suspicious attachments in evidence. The seal of the bottle was unbroken. The contents smelled of gin. A drop splashed on my skin didn't hurt at all. I took a little sip, and the gin ran thrillingly down my gullet and into my seedy innards. With greedy excitement I tipped the little bottle upside down and felt the liquid rush through me, its fire warming my guts. I suddenly felt it was one of those rare good-to-be-alive days, when everything goes right. I scrambled to the top of a nearby rubbish heap, feeling on top of the world. Lustily I vented a cubic metre of wind, whistled a few bars of "Jumping Jack Flash" and admired the view. Weather-wise it wasn't a bad day at all, only about eighty per cent toxic cloud, with inspiring glimpses of blue sky and occasional shafts of smoggy sunbeams. A family of rats emerged from inside a dead baby which someone had abandoned on a nearby mattress and I cheerily threw the empty bottle at them. The bottle missed and smashed with a merry tinkle on the burned-out skeleton of a pram. The rats glanced at me with weary indifference, then slouched off in the direction of Westminster. I scrambled back down the tangled mound of cold ashes, rotting vegetables and heaped black sacks. I'd almost reached the ground when I slipped on some cabbage leaves and went crashing sideways against some sacks. The weight of my body caused one to split open with a sudden bang, as if it contained something putrefying and gassy. Out from the split came a a slow ooze of cold chicken curry. And not just curry: borne on the sludge-coloured tide was a hard unidentifiable object. The curry was what you might call a bit high, and dappled with patches of green mould here and there, but you soon learn not to be fastidious in The Dump. I squatted excitedly on some back numbers of *The Economist* and began scooping the curry into my mouth. "There," I said to myself, "I just *knew* it was going to be a good day." The gin had given me quite an appetite and I tucked in heartily with both hands. As I ate I gradually worked my way towards the mysterious curry-covered object. Finally I pulled it out and began to lick off the curry to see what lay underneath. As soon as I'd lifted it free from the curry I had a pretty good idea from the double-barrelled shape what I was going to find and I was right. It was a pair of binoculars! Not just any binoculars either but Zeiss binoculars, with a X7 magnification. "How on earth does a pair of binoculars end up in a rubbish sack coated in chicken curry?" you might wonder. No use asking me. Let me just say that that one of the intriguing and interesting things about life on The Dump is the strange things that get thrown away for no apparent reason, not to mention the strange juxtaposition of things which don't belong together at all. You get a real sense of life's rich variety and mystery, living in The Dump. In fact you probably end up knowing more about life among The Barbarians than The

Barbarians do themselves. Sometimes I must admit I've been quite shocked at the things I've discovered – pornographic magazines wrapped inside Church Diocesan Newsletters, used condoms concealed inside jam jars, obscene photographs hidden away in abandoned handbags and (once) a discarded Scout Master's uniform. Not to mention intimate letters containing graphic and astonishing descriptions and remarks which might have shamed the Marquis de Sade, all jostling together with mountains of empty gin bottles, empty whisky bottles, empty beer bottles, empty bottles of port and Martini Bianco and cider and Cointreau and sherry and brandy and vodka. You name it, The Dump will have it. Somewhere. Sometimes you get the feeling that all The Barbarians are interested in is sex and alcohol. Sometimes I think the only other place where you must learn about the truth of things is down in the city sewers, in among the shit and the gin bottles and the thousand-and-one things that guilty shamefaced folk flush down the lav when no one else is about. People make me puke but I don't have the sort of temperament ever to become an Apathetic. Admittedly I sometimes feel bilious, admittedly sometimes I nearly lose my head. Once I burst into tears over a cistern of goldfishes. But the thing I like about The Dump is that just when you start to get the glooms something turns up out of the blue to make it seem worth going on. Like that long-desired pair of binoculars. I licked the binos clean and was impressed by their appearance. They were a heavy, handsome black pair. Holding them I felt a real sense of power. I had a hunch they were probably German and had once been used in vitally important espionage work. I reached into my pocket for a tissue, gave the lenses a final polish and raised them to my eyes. Amazing, truly amazing. I could see the carcase of a rotting dog in vivid detail, even though it must have been three-hundred yards away. I could even make out the feverish activity of scores of grey-white maggots as they burrowed and frolicked in the bloodied blue-brown gash of the creature's burst stomach. I could see the whirr of tiny wings and the shimmer of sunlight on the bead-like bodies of bluebottles circling and spiralling amid the rising fumes of putrefaction. I was thrilled. I gave a little whoop of delight. The gin still jigged in my veins, bringing out the impulsive side of my nature. I decided then and there to set out at once in search of visual adventures. It is always a little hard to know in which direction to go in The Dump. One way is much the same as another – an endless uneven vista of rubbish heaps, sprawled garbage and broken machines illumined by spurts of emerging subterranean fire and shadowed by dark familiar toxic clouds. I stood there for some minutes, my heart thumping with expectation. Should I head South, in the direction of the Isle of Dogs? West, towards Tottenham and Finsbury Park? To the East the M11 beckoned, highway to the cloisters of Cambridge, the Fens, the rush of traffic going up and down the Great North Road. Northward lay reservoirs, bird sanctuaries, lonely islands, the call of the wild... Or how about South West, to Penge? Perhaps it was spring, perhaps I should try – Nique ta Mère! – Paris. Pop across on le smouldering Shuttle and commit verbal outrage against public authority. Or piss in the Panthéon. Or instead head for Carthage. It would be nice to head for Carthage to see if it still exists. There's a rumour, a suburb of Tumour. Eh? Or perhaps Lacedaemon. Or Zug. Zug sounds like the sort of place someone like me would enjoy. So many choices, so many miles of unending, fresh rubbish to explore. My appetite for travel was often whetted by the travel brochures I'd come across in The Dump. There's nothing quite so pleasurable as squatting in a warm ditch gazing at pictures of tanned young women stretched out invitingly in skimpy bikinis on deserted sandy beaches. I have spent many happy hours turning the pages of glossy brochures, absent-mindedly pinching my fleas, or pleasurably picking the crispy limestone-like formations inside my nostrils, or using the narrow end of a biro's cap to scrape the sportive threadworm from their cavortings and convulsions around the plump crater's lip of my hot, reeking anus, all the while excitedly comparing the merits of Poros and Zakynthos, of Agistri and Skopelos, of Rhodes or Kos. To head for Corfu or Crete? – an agonising choice. Would the climate damage my parasites? – the cretinous blonde girl in the travel agent's would be, I felt certain, quite unable to tell me. She would press a concealed button and the manager, a sleek bryclreemed thug named Den, would escort me out of the complex. Pity. I used to love going in and helping myself to a clutch of luminous brochures (no thanks, just browsing). I suppose it's because a travel brochure brings out the existentialist in all of us. A travel brochure makes you face up to iron choices and the randomness of destiny. I have spent months pouring over the relative merits of large Greek villages offering friendly hospitality and close to bustling Rhodes Town while still retaining their character, apartments in the centre of Ixia ideally located just 345 metres from the beach and 250 metres from the nearest disco, comfortable two-bedroom apartments with kitchenette (cooking rings and fridge), bathroom with shower and that all-important w.c., and rooms on the main road about 470 metres from the main street of Falikaris with a disco just across the road and a nearby supermarket. My idea of hell, if you must. Vomiting youths, stinking traffic, girls shrieking, the moronic electronic all-night throb of idiot music. Sometimes I used to scoop up half a dozen fleas and bring them into my agonizing decision-making. I'd line them up and watch them hop across the grids in the brochure's table of preferences. For some reason Lively After Dark almost always came out the winner, closely followed by Good Food. Local History, Great for Families, Good Beaches and Variety of Watersports never did very well. But many's the day when I wasn't in the mood for Greece, no matter how louring the sky. Stuff Lindos, a lovely magical place which everyone should see at least once, with the formidable walls of a castle looming over the town halfway up a steep rocky hill, with sand beach and harbour below and the remains of a temple to Athena on top of the rock and a quite breathtaking view over the village to the turd-dotted sea. As often occurred at the end of a dizzying perusal of brochures, I closed my eyes, spun on my heel – and fell flat in the mud (my heel had fallen off). So many choices in life! Once I took a cabbage into town to buy some cloisters but today I decided to head in the direction of my nose. Always a good idea if the existential grandeur of available choices threatens to overwhelm. My nose, half-immersed in a sort of grey sludge I instantly recognised as wet ash, was pointing approximately south-west.

Right, I thought. Penge it is. I staggered to my feet, snorting a few times to get the muck out of my nostrils. I made half-hearted efforts to scrape some of the slime off my blazer and trousers just in case I bumped into someone I might need to impress. Then, slinging the binocular straps over my right shoulder I set off across a grey ocean of waste paper and smouldering ashes. I walked all day without meeting a soul. All day I sang to myself, or whistled, or hummed. "Hallelujah, I'm a Bum!" "Though cowards flinch and traitors sneer..." "A great while ago the world began..." Etcetera. The sun was blotted out by cloud and it became a typical Dump day, grey and empty. Periodically I stopped by small mountains of garbage and scrambled to the top. Raising the binoculars to my eyes I scanned the smoky distances for signs of life or interesting rubbish. Apart from crowds of lively rats and the occasional distant emaciated dog nothing moved. As the afternoon waned I found shelter beneath a mahogany table. Like Madame de Clèves I was not in a state to sleep. I say mahogany, for all I know it was oak. The only wood I have ever been able to identify is balsa wood, from my childhood glider days. Let me simply say that it was everything I imagined mahogany to be. The table was dark brown, knotty and still had an inspiring shine, as if refusing to be bowed down by adversity. It was a table that had seen better days. It had probably spent many happy years in Buckinghamshire, weighed down by fine food and wine and sprayed with Lord Jenkins' spittle and his fat-bottomed, plump-bellied, florid-faced very agreeable political wisdom, not to mention a splatter of freshly lisped anecdotes concerning the contemporary press. Then its owners had decided to replace it, and now here it was, all alone in a waste land of ash and rain and smoke. Somewhere along the line it had lost a leg, and as I crouched beneath it I watched it sway a little in the breeze and heard the rattle of its leaves. Some black rubbish sacks were conveniently to hand, and I split them open with my knife. There is nothing like a good rummage through someone's rubbish just before nightfall. The tease of enigmatic scraps. *Whatever happened to Dorcas?* scrawled in an agonised hand. What can we say? The pressure in the script is erratic. The t bar crossing is wavy. The westward swing of the p and the shrivelled d give the game away. I see lurches of mood, a powerful mother, instability, a yearning for islands, stamp collecting, a fondness for Tolstoy. As for *Buses back every hour, quarter past the hour at Dollarton. Transfer to 910 at 2nd Narrows Bridge.* Note the phallus-shaped upper loops. This is the work of a man of deranged politics and abnormal sexual appetites. Ripped pages, scraps. Sheer bliss. *This is the story of a man, one who was never at a loss.* Once, I remember, I actually found a tin of condensed milk which some sweet, mischievous child must have tossed into Mummy's swing-bin, doubtless in revenge for some harsh parental admonition. But this time there were no treats in store, merely cold chips, used tissues, empty baked-bean cans and the torn-up remains of someone's insurance policy which stated in a quaint copperplate font – don't ask me which one, fonts were never one of my strong points – that the policy did not cover loss or damage directly or indirectly occasioned by or happening through or in consequence of war, invasion, acts of foreign enemies, hostilities (whether war be declared or not), civil war, rebellion, insurrection, terrorism or military or usurped power, riot or civil commotion nor legal liability of whatsoever nature directly or indirectly caused by or contributed to, by, or arising from ionising radiations or contamination by radioactivity from any irradiated nuclear fuel or from any nuclear waste from the combustion of nuclear fuel or the radioactive toxic explosive or other hazardous properties of any explosive nuclear assembly or nuclear component thereof, or abduction by intergalactic aliens whether miniscule, gigantic, slimy, fanged, winged or of leathery appearance, from any zone of the universe whatsoever, not excluding parallel universes, worm holes, black holes, yellow supergiants, double stars, white dwarfs, orange giants, Cepheid-type variables, large globular clusters of all classes of stellar luminosity, planets and moons, including The Moon, whether or not at gibbous phase. All of which perked me up no end as I reflected upon what The Barbarians had coming to them. It would be no use them coming to me for sympathy, no way. And on this happy thought I gulped down the cold chips, used two of the rubbish sacks as a pillow and fell asleep under the possibly mahogany table, its leaves still rattling gently in the evening breeze. A trail of cartoon zeds emanated from my lice-infested scalp. Inane rhymes rattled away. *Little Peter Rabbit had a prickle in his prick, so he pulled it and pulled it and – ooh!* And Thanatos. Thanatos in the darks outside, Thanatos gathering in the hollow boring afternoons, Thanatos in the empty mornings, the empty bed. Inanition! The old noble endeavour to be heard above – pardon – the wind. Pope John Paul II crawled across the floor. I expected him to look a faded yellow, like old yolk on a tie. The spectacle of a large hairless humanoid came as a considerable shock. He was kneeling, naked, in front of a crumpled picture of Jayne Mansfield, vigorously massaging his inguinal region. Beyond his wizened buttocks I caught a glimpse of the crosses that run from Tata Mai Lau down to Lake Tacitolu, near where the stinking old man said Mass in 1989. I turned away in disgust and decided to go trampolining in Australia. Somebody said something about Aztecs. The educational system ensured that my child learned the dates of wars, the surnames of portly statesmen. Australia? Australia is formed of a layer of honey and dead Aborigines. These rest on sheets of cardboard several miles thick. For understandable reasons the study of geology is restricted to an élite. Question. For ten points. Is Australia the shape of (i) a stain (ii) the damaged remains of the fossilised skull of a hitherto undiscovered dinosaur (iii) the mildewed pear we discovered in Jane's kitchen, after her death? Bigger and better trampolines are being invented all the time. On the best you can bounce more than six miles into the air. The blue skies are filled with young, healthy, streamlined figures passing hither and thither. Sarah sniffed her scrapings. "These are the droppings of a postmodernist," she said, with an air of knowledgeable authority. Mandeville broke in. "Have you had" – he paused. He looked at me keenly. "Have you had any strange experiences?" I told him about the earlier episode when someone tried to shoot me. "But of course," I explained, "it was just an hallucination. Probably a chemical reaction in that tin of condensed milk I ate." "No," he said. "Not an hallucination." "Not an hallucination?" "By no means. You were experiencing that most dreadful of all forces.

85

Worse than a raging storm. Worse than tempest or typhoon. Worse than an elephant's fart. Worse than a Japanese earthquake. Worse than the blast of a bomb." I waited expectantly. He did not disappoint me. "Revision!" he said. "The creative process. Deletions, tinkerings, rewritings. 'Silver Blaze,' say. An old story. '"We are going well," he remarked, looking out of the train window and glancing at his watch. "Our rate at present is fifty-three and a half miles an hour." I sighed, realising the seriousness of my poor friend's condition. "Yes, yes of course we are," I said, soothingly. "The telegraph posts upon this line are sixty yards apart!" "Yes, yes. Sixty yards apart. Of course. Clever of you to have had the foresight to measure them." My poor friend's descent into madness had been evident for some months and was a source of continual concern to everyone who knew him. Earlier in the year he had emerged from a polling booth, grinning like a monkey and shouting that he had just voted Conservative in order to get the economy moving again. On another occasion he had been distinctly heard to say that the royal family were a credit to the nation. As a doctor I was unhappily aware that there had recently been some severe outbreaks of Delusion in the south, and my friend's case was the worst I had come across. "I am afraid that I shall have to go," he had remarked that morning at breakfast. "Go! Where to?" "To Dartmoor – to King's Pyland." A furtive glance at a gazetteer of Britain revealed that there was no such place, but I decided to play along with my friend's little fantasy. "I should be most happy to accompany you," I replied, reaching for my bag of sedatives and tranquillizers. "Good. Your time will not be misspent. There are points about this case which promise to make it an absolutely unique one. No one should be surprised that this is the one topic of conversation throughout the length and breadth of England!" "No one," I echoed blandly, disturbed to hear my friend talking like a journalist on one of the cheaper newspapers.' And so on," Mandeville gasped, as I hurriedly erased him. Night fell like all the other nights. Like the night we drove up Bredon Hill. The night I saw movement on the step at the back of that Cotswold pub. Cockroaches, gleaming like creatures from Mare Acidalium. The night at Brindisi. The Athens night. The night in Seattle. The night at Claremont Road. The night you were caught in the draught from an unfinished draft. So to speak. Between drafts, yes. That bullet was real. I am in terrible pain. I bleed. I need a nurse. A nurse? Nurse Molly Ffunntt. A sexy little thing. Black hair, cheeky eyes. Fishnet stockings. Breasts like melons. Her eyes conspired with her armpits to give her away. Asking for it, she was. Begging for it. Dripping. Reeking. Juicy seaweed slopping on a brimming tide. Wanting it, over and over again. Acrobatic. Broad-minded. Interested in experiment. Christ. What? I've got an erection! My first for seventeen years! It will drive me mad, I know it will. I haven't even seen a woman all year. I mopped my face. I stared anxiously at the tumour welling up in my lower midriff. Grotesque. "Wake up for Sharp's sake!" a voice screeched. "You haven't listened to a word I've been saying, have you? I can see you've repaired to a brown study. I thought I'd made it crystal clear. The bullet was from the first draft. It was real. Then he spared you. For something altogether worse, I wouldn't mind betting. And by the way, you didn't drink any condensed milk." "I swear I did! I remember it vividly. It had a white label. I searched for days before I found a suitable tin-opener." "You don't know your own mind. You're talking nonsense." "Oh really?" "You'll see. You'll find out. Until this bloody thing is published we are all at risk. Anything can happen at any time. Death. Mutilation. An operation performed by a bungling amateur." He shuddered. "An operation?" "He bought a second-hand book about surgery when he was on holiday in Dorset. A terrifying thing." "Who did? What holiday in Dorset? What on earth are you talking about?" "For God's sake keep your voice down! He might hear us!" "Who?" "Shut up. I'm going. I never saw you before. I hate you. If you suddenly find yourself requiring a Hodgen's splint don't say I didn't bloody warn you. And even when the book's out you won't be safe!" "What do you mean?" "Remember Henry James! Not satisfied with the published version, oh no. A right one for the scissors and ink, he was. And remember what happened to the end of *Great Expectations*. Not to mention *The Magus*. Some of these bloody writers are no better than Hollywood producers. They'll do anything. Sometimes to suit themselves, sometimes to please the punters. For example, John Barth's first book, can't remember the title. Not to mention what might have happened to *Under the Volcano*. Lowry was quite prepared to countenance cuts for a paperback edition. Cuts! I ask you! Admittedly by 1952 the poor sod was getting desperate. So don't say I haven't warned you. Don't think your genitals are your own, they're not. You're never safe in this game." My hands dropped downward, forming a protective cup around my crotch. He was raving. All the same, best not to take chances. I watched him run out of sight, skipping along as if in extreme discomfort from spermatorrhoea. About twenty minutes later I heard a scream of pain followed by a soft of PHUT! A greyish pillar of muck erupted into the sky from beyond the horizon. Whether this event had anything to do with the previous sentences remains uncertain. I hurried away, extracted a shiny brochure from my rags and relaxed beside a malodorous mound of putrefying pilchards. Four-score dead eyes gazed listlessly at me. *What could be better than a weekend in Amsterdam? Don't miss De Pijp. The perfect spot to observe Amsterdammers going about their business*. What a disgusting suggestion. Why should I nourish a desire to observe zipped bilinguals going about their malodorous business? The notion sickens me. I shall go nowhere near the Low Countries. A filthy, depraved, drug-ridden brackish place, by all accounts. The sickly reek of tulips would make me puke. I would end up in swordfights with belligerent windmills. The same goes for everywhere else. Three nights in New York? Hell. I do not wish to Discover Turkey or anywhere else. To mooch around fountains and piazzas is a loathsome prospect. The faintest thought of shopping sprees or lazy canal trips brings on a severe migraine. I have a vampire's attitude to sunlight. Stuff the glorious views of the Palatine or the Castelo de Sao Jorge. Who wants to waste a second of their lives gawking at Sainte Chapelle and the Palais de Justice? I wish to avoid places Where Art Meets Architecture. Balls to the Museum of Classical Art (a load of Bosch). Balls to the places where PoMo style meets gothic elegance. Faced by La Casa Pedrera I would only yawn. Force me on to the Laederstraede and I would flee, propelled by explosive farts, bored and unwell. I can do without The Liberties or the Alfama. I shudder to think of the ideal weather conditions which can be experienced at Aqaba. The very word resort makes me resort to the little room. As mother always called it. I detest scheduled seat configurations. The very idea of an itinerary makes me sick. I can do without a walk through the siq. Bugger Belém. Bugger the monumental arch and the royal tombs. Bugger the Mosteiro dos Jerónimos with its marvellously elaborate cloister. Sod the turn-of-the-century stucco and impressive wooden panelling. Sod the Schönbrunn palace, summer residence of the imperial family. Air-conditioning, yech. Gentle spring sunshine brings me out in a cold sweat. Fresh air, exercise, horror. Company? Horror. As for the food! Defecate the lot, the Viennese patisseries, the roast pork and sauerkraut, the grilled prawns, the vanilla ice with brandy-soaked raisins resembling a blend of grout and rabbit shit. The very thought of the glamour of the Côte d'Azur chills me to the marrow. I can manage at best a spark of interest in Les Lanternes des Morts but I shall never visit them, no. I do not wish to get on, let alone get off, the beaten track. Just leave me alone, will you! In my warm ditch. My most memorable ditch contained an intriguing excavation about the shape of a large ham. In it I read in its entirety *Hamlet*, which I had only once seen performed, by a hambone. Its widest space at the innermost end. The hole through which you entered was the narrowest part, the knuckle of the ham. I masked the hole with an armful of oxidised paper. The size of the hole itself I reduced with rectangular blocks of language. Scraps of Tolstoy, Turgenev, whatever came to hand. Dostoyevsky was never much help. Each block was faced with dirt, rubbish and leftovers. The small remaining aperture allowed foul air to pass both ways. Compressed alongside gigantic Molly, whom I had lured into my hidey-hole with the promise of jelly, I found myself kneaded into the swelling thigh of the ham. I had expected to suffer from cold but the earth was dry and surprisingly warm. Molly's huge body exuded heat, moisture and bursts of succulent, bubbling gas. The atmosphere quickly became more than tropical. Her coarse pubic hair grated against my stomach like sandpaper.

She munched her jelly contentedly, smiling tenderly at my pitiful wrinkled drooping organ. Despite our best efforts it refused to budge. "Not since—" I began, but she pressed a finger to her lips and winked. Incidentally, my mind is going. It may just be age. When I was tested I had the top score of anyone on the Holmes and Rahe social readjustment rating scale. I was advised I would never, ever readjust. "Interested in brass rubbings?" I asked the shrink. I know the type, sneaking up beside girls on the tube, muttering "Dost want ter walk wi' me?" and "I could die for the touch of a woman like thee" and "Eh! Tha'rt lovely to touch!" and "Why it's suicide for a man to go in there!" and "Sibelius's Fourth Symphony is a veritable White Dwarf in the musical firmament!" and "'Appen as yer'd come ter th' cottage one time" and similar drivel. I am sick of women. Of bipeds in general. Give me solitude and a nice warm ditch any day. Are you, like me, nervously aware of the fallibility of engines? You can guess how carefully I chewed over what I was to tell mother. What's that? Good news! Bubonic plague has returned to New York! Cholera has also made a comeback! Word spread. Across The Dump a cheer went up. Schadenfreude is a delicious emotion. We savoured the thought. The big apple – rotten to the core! Next morning after breakfast I scrutinised the climate. Breakfast? A rind, the creature unidentifiable. I sucked it, dreaming of three martinis and a bowl of nembutal. It was a windy day. One of those days when tired butterflies depart for California. One of those days when a filthy old man crouches behind the hut in the park, humming the Agitato from Schnittke's third string quartet. One of those days when you are liable to encounter degenerate centrist fragments of the Fourth International. One of those days when it seems more important than ever to touch your toes. Tone up those muscles! Avoid lapsing back into a form of Second Internationalism! One of those days when you encounter the abbreviation CUN'T. As in *I won't say it to you 'cause you cun't understand it*. As disgusting a piece of innuendo as you could possibly hope to come across in a book about pubescent boys. And by Richmal Crompton too! I shall write and protest. At least, I would if I could ever breach The Great Barrier and get back to the land of the Barbarians. Ah, The

Dump, The Dump. Shut off from the outside world as if at the request of a Chief Constable and granted by the Home Secretary both equally concerned that a trespassory assembly might occur without the consent of a member of the ruling class, resulting in serious disruption to the concerns of bigots, capitalists and/or Conservatives under Section 14(2) of the Public Order Act (1986). At times like a battlefield, like Passchendaele, or the broken temples, the wastes, after the Tet offensive. Eh? Eh? Easy now, Robinson. Calm down. Your face bright red. Your hair, what's left of it, lets drop a few more grey tufts. You need a break, sport. A brisk stroll in an imaginary park. An invigorating circumnavigation of the spectral lake. Pause amid the Siberian breeze to admire the defecating ducks, the howling sobbing children, the screaming mother, the hatchet-faced warden, the cretinous bourgeoises towing their shit-bloated quadrupeds past the NO DOGS notice. Easy, easy. Time for your tumbler of Bénédictine. The bouts of deafness get worse. Sleep, it is a blessed thing. Until woken by the traffic, the mental hammering, the tilt and spin of the planet. A terrifying thing to be whirled around all the time at 70,000 mph on a lump of rock! Pinned down as I am by gravity. Given a risible breathing space. Time for a fizzing mugful of health salts specially formulated to ease upset stomachs, *Angst*, indigestion, biliousness, constipation and acute dehydration. Just the thing at one thirty in the morning to flush away the mouthslime, that parched middle-of-the-desert sensation, that you've-done-it-again-you-fool feeling. Drink before effervescence subsides. No sweat. What's that? For heartburn. Heartburn! It will take more than two spoonfuls and half a glass of water to put out that inferno, I can tell you. I feel awful. Sick and ill. Cramps in my chest. Too ghastly for. Words. But I'll. Try. I'll do my. Miserable best. It horrifies me to think that the duty of the peritoneum is to anchor the intestines to the front of the backbone and to convey blood-vessels and nerves to the walls of the intestine. It disgusts me to discover that the muscular coat has fibres of muscle arranged lengthwise on the outer surface and round and round on the inside. I don't think I can bear to hear any more about that loose tissue between the muscle and the mucous coat or details relating to that inner mucous layer which contains the various digestive glands. It is nauseating to contemplate the folds of the mucuous membrane of the small intestine. Or the various types of glands opening on the inner surface of the intestine. Speak to me not of succus entericus. Eh? The yellow alkaline fluid, you oaf! It blends the juices of these glands. Whisper not of the multitude of very small projections which cover the surface of the inner side of the small intestine. Never mention digestion, never tell of how lumps of ingested matter (food, if you must) pass from the stomach into the duodenum. A hideous fate, to be swamped by bile and pancreatic juice. Screen me from knowledge of how the dissolved portions are rapidly absorbed by the mucous membrane while the unabsorbed parts pass onwards to the large bowel, of how these savaged lumps from the small intestine enter the large intestine through the ileo-caecal valve and are then subjected (poor things!) to brutal peristaltic movements, not to mention rhythmic segmentation, until for some (vile thought!) putrefaction occurs. Tell no one that the contents of the large intestine are bacteria, bile, mucus, unabsorbed food and excess of digestive juices. That the bacteria form nearly half of the solids excreted. That the colour of shit is mostly due to the bile. That the presence of food in the stomach has a marked reflex action in making the rectum contract. That this tendency is most marked when food is placed into a stomach which is completely empty. That the most suitable time to void the bowels and send a cosmic stench surging through the household is directly after that buttered, pockmarked crumpet. "The bowel is a creature of habits and to make it work with maximum efficiency it should be made to contract and expel its contents at precisely the same time every day," said Stevenson. "Experts believe 8.37 a.m. (Greenwich Mean Time) produces the best results. The rectum can also be important when dealing with very ill people. There is some evidence to show that such persons can be kept alive by pumping a glucose solution up their arse. This treatment is very popular with passive homosexuals." Some mornings, when he walked, Stevenson felt that one leg was shorter than the other. His thin lips incessantly twisted into a malevolent smile. He was an expert on runes. He could talk for hours about R F S H F + (a rough, crude, inappropriate transcription) the earliest runic carving in England. Sixteen hundred years old! Apparently. Found in the cremation cemetery at Caistor, just outside Norwich. Carved on the ankle-bone of a roe deer. Its text, says Professor Page, reads *raïhan*. Which means "roe deer". Apparently. Far away, on the shore at Selsey, two strips of gold were washed ashore. The rune on one reads *brnrn*. This, says Professor Page, "does not look as if it ever meant anything". Seventeen million dead last year, not bad, not bad at all, eh? As for me, you. Be patient. The game will soon be up. Half an hour at best. I stir my dregs. Call me a whirl-brain that talks whatever comes uppermost. Observe my alternating layers of muck. Muck? A paste comprised of mud, soot, cement dust and chicken blood. Encrusted upon my skin from brow to chin. Only natural in my condition you might think. Owing to the perpetual clouds of thick black smoke. A richly toxic smoke emanating from burning tyres, incinerated plastic, foam-filled furniture, you name it. Apart from hygiene nuts and a handful of new arrivals, everyone in The Dump is black as sin (as mother used to say). Indeed, members of the ethnic community are often surprised to discover that they feel quite at home in The Dump. Racial discrimination is unknown. The only white people you see in The Dump are the new arrivals and The Soapers. No matter how trim and fragrant they might be when they first arrive, by the end of their first day the new arrivals are as grimy and foul-smelling as the next person. Unless, of course, they arrive clutching a tablet of soap. Soap is especially prized by members of deranged religious cults, who scrub themselves like lunatics. Often they foam at the mouth. They dream of a new home in one of eight available styles (Classical, Tudor, Georgian, Neo-Colonial, Imperial, Chic French, Enchanted Greek or Machiavellian), the nice sun shining down from a nice clear sky. A blue sky. A winnowing wind, small gnats engaged in hybridized discourse among the river sallows, drowsy tinklings, blushing roses, a stern Lawrentian rainbow in the russell sky. It was on such a day that I met the old man with an inexhaustible fund of stories. The story of the bucket and the beautiful woman. The story of the old man and the missing comb. The story of the princess and the cod. The story of the long queues at the local supermarket. The story of Sibelius's silence. The story of G's forty winks. The story of the traffic warden. The story of the Great Trigonometrical Survey of India. The story of the de Sade study aid with excellent illustrations drawing attention to difficult passages, common areas of difficulty and areas which carry most marks in any examination. The story of the important letter that disappeared. The story of Louise Bryant's six months. The story of the trader who lived on Konkumba island. The story of the young man who flew to a strange city and had many remarkable adventures there. The story of Dobson. Dobson was a moody fellow who did not much like people, other than loose women, whom he loved to shake and jangle, cocking his ear and grinning. Sometimes he brooded about the silent compulsion of economic relations, sometimes about commodity fetishism. Sometimes he'd shriek: "Storm the Reality Studios!" And so the years go by. This is a keyboard, that is a window. This is not a mountain, it is my thumb. Over there is the fireplace and the red train. This is my llama. This is my biscuit. These are my piglets. I have seven. I am not. You are not. He is not. She is not. It is not. Berwald is not. He died on April 3. Kjerulf died on August 11. Lalo died on April 22. Chabrier died on September 13. Lekeu died on January 21. Fibich died on October 15. "The sea is hungrier than death," asserted Swinburne, East Anglia. We are not. You are not. They are not, especially Plomer. Who are you? How are you? All is tickle with me. Eh? What are you all? *In the background – behind the affably grinning old gentlemen, the fashionable dandies, the elegantly infirm old widows and the perfumed beauties in their cashmeres, ostrich feathers, and garlands of flowers and diamonds – stood the constable with his waterproof coat, greasy oilskin hat and truncheon – the reverse side of the coin.* Is that right? How many books are in my head? How many windows are there in your mind? Please leave at once. I at once cried out. He knew at once what had happened. Anyone suffering from diarrhoea alternating with constipation should consult a doctor at once. Coat lightly with flour and laugh. Avoid Cairo. "And?" said

Dobson. "And that was that." "Ah, well. You know what they say." "What do they say?" "Man is born unto trouble, as the sparks fly upward." "Being old and full of gas." "Fancy! I hadn't heard." Flauerbouiller! They yearned for the legible. Night fell. A mist came down. And behold, there came a great wind from the wilderness, and smote the four corners of the structure, collapsing it. They are all gone now. Little more than ghosts. Bare bones. As for little me. I look like a human porpoise. Or did, once. In my heyday. All gone. I only am escaped alone to tell thee. Then there were other times, times I'd be feeling rather gloomy and downcast when a sudden streak of cheerfulness would break in and off I'd go, over the sludge and the mass graves, humming some such tune as "Jerusalem" or "Land of Hope and Glory" or perhaps chirpily whistling "Roses Are Blooming in Picardy". Or perhaps I'd overhear the tunes of others, a robust ex-postman greatly resembling Dirk Bogarde crooning "I'm Laughing On The Outside But Crying On The Inside", a nuclear physicist with a blooming complexion bellowing something soulful by Norma Egstrom. A waif humming "The Tennessee Waltz". "Cold, Cold Heart". Next I tried to cry but could only raise a squeak like a bat. Beneath me the powdery crackle of broken glass, quite distinct from the faint distant throb of amplified sounds predominantly characterised by the emission – the emission! – of a succession of repetitive beats. Sorry, didn't I mention the mass graves before? I've got so much to tell you I can't possibly hope to remember everything, can I? Be fair. The Dump is such a stimulating environment there are bound to be things I've forgotten to tell you about and which just slip out by accident. The mass graves. Her smile. My poor old dick, for example, as the woman says in Peckinpah's last. Peckinpah's thirteenth I wrote in the first draft, quite overlooking, as you should, *The Deadly Companions*. Hollywood! Conversation was somewhat spasmodic for the next half hour. "We'll get the data hot off the line. Art's coming with us." "We can always leave early if we get bored." "You never know where you'll end up." "I've seen her somewhere I'm sure. Who is she?" "Do you mean you don't know?" "Fragmentary in the extreme. Nobody can fit the facts together." Hollywood, yes. I work there, you know.

Really? Yeah. In animation. Mostly. I sketch chipmunks. But sometimes I work on screenplays. The doctor turned. "Why don't you go home. You can, you know." "I'm waiting for my hat." Her smile, her smile. In that long fresh light of waning April days which affects us often with a sadness sharper than the greyest days of autumn. As for the mass graves. The mass graves represent quite an interesting conundrum (a word Dobson taught me). You do not come across them very often, and always by accident, but nevertheless they are there (although I have often met Wanderers who indignantly deny their existence just because they have wandered for years and never come across one). They are usually discovered when half a dozen people get together and decide to have an organized excavation. A description? Pull the other one. If I don't get this manuscript off soon it may go up in smoke. Or be found in fragments. Worse, in multiple drafts. Next thing you'll have P zealously promoting the Z version, while Q defends the A-text and R holds fast to his B-edition and S prefers the C version. Or worse, reduced to a solitary scorched sheet. Like the blackened certificate I found one day. A very nice, very pretty certificate, with some lovely gold scroll around the margins. *THIS CERTIFICATE DOES NOT* it began *DOES NOT* it repeated *cover any consequence whether direct or indirect of foreign enemy hostilities (whether war be declared or not) civil war civil commotion rebellion revolution insurrection nationalised industry or military or usurped power or any consequence of aviation including defecation or urination royal or ordinary or mental illness or wilfully self-inflicted injury or illness or desperate headaches or cycling, motor-cycling, walking, hopping, swimming, pot-holing, nose-picking, fishing, hang-gliding, the breaking of wind, belching, parachuting, winter sports, summer sports, copulation, onanism, cunnilingus, buggery, bestiality, skin-diving, fetishism, transvestism, leather garments, thongs, intoxicating liquor, drugs or drug-addiction, and especially NOT drugs prescribed and directed by a qualified registered medical practitioner for the treatment of venereal disease.* One day, holding my valuable certificate, I shall drop down a hole without warning, a sixty-foot hole with barbed metal at the bottom, treacherously concealed by cardboard, perhaps a loose scattering of ash. Perhaps I will wake up in the Joy House shelter, Milwaukee. "All of a sudden, you think everything's okay, and then boom!" said Cynthia Geiger, who blames herself for believing she would get a warning notice before her welfare payments were docked. State and county officials vigorously deny that Wisconsin's aggressive welfare reform programme is responsible for the city's rise in homelessness. Or perhaps Indonesia. The Foreign Office minister said, "If water cannon is used to try to stop peaceful demonstrators, that is of course totally unacceptable; if it is used to stop rioters, that may be acceptable." Or perhaps I will be caught in one of the blow-outs, incinerated, or (more probably), just horribly burned, causing me to run here and there, soaked in fire, before collapsing on an old sofa, my skin hanging from me like seaweed. Unseen. In a flash. Goodbye! Night... Sweet dreams. A wheel started to turn round in my head and when I looked at the moon I saw that it was rotating in time. Goodbye. Hello, what's this? Scrap of old newspaper. Mrs Gillian Shephard, the Agriculture Minister, said she saw no problem in dealing with neo-fascists. "They are democratically elected," she said. Ah, the press! Ennui. Fatigue. Boredom. These are the dangers of life on The Dump. If it wasn't for the newspapers we would probably all succumb. It is the newspapers that alert us to the outside world, that give meaning to our poor miserable days. It is not a good thing to have a parochial attitude. Ennui must be fought, vigorously. Baudelaire must be blotted out. Dolour of mind and discomfort of flesh must be resisted. There must be no asking after Mr Campbell or George Hardt or the Snow Bird. One must never say, "By the way, what's become of Claude Fessenden?" What becomes of anyone? Older, wrinklier, more fragile, patches of dry white flaking skin breaking out at the tips of your elbows, across your kneecaps, in patches on your back. Wind, and worse. The broken sheds, the heartbreak, the dews at even. Thickest dark. The slow clock ticking. And then... The gray-eyed morn. One morning, a morning when I might otherwise have decided to stay in my ditch, dozing (or worse), I came across an old newspaper which alerted me to the fact that I was not merely an inhabitant of The Dump. I was also A YEW-ROPE-EEEANN. As fit as an international flea, I ran along a foul-smelling ridge of imported vegetable refuse. Someone had scattered old German tyres there like stepping-stones and I hopped athletically from one to the next. Then, suddenly, all the enthusiasm seemed to go out of me. I stopped, got off the tyre upon which I was trembling and clambered down a slope of rotting apples to a shady dell where mushrooms were growing. I muttered to myself, a most satisfying mutter, then paused a moment for reflection. I considered the career of Courbet. Tick! tick! tick! Incidentally, I wish to deny absolutely the rumours about the disease in the temporal lobe of my brain. Total rot! As for those concerning my anus. The misrepresentation is fundamental. Tick! tick! tick! Autoscopic hallucination? Nonsense! Pass me that telescopic sight at once! Nightmare on Elm Street? Hold on, I won't be a tick. A quick scratch of my burning scalp, then time to take aim! Time to take stock. Of everything. Especially the. Not forgetting that. And above all. Tick! tick! tick! A pair of jackdaws dressed in trim, clean lounge suits were pecking at a garden tub. I lay down beside a heap of fractured plastic flowerpots and felt a great sense of ANXIETY surge through me. To what extent, I wondered, should the direction of improvements in the welfare state be halted or changed in the interests of controlling public spending and improving competitiveness by reducing business costs? Is it possible to engineer a switch of taxation which would prove beneficial to the environment? Can the European Union keep pace with the next industrial revolution of information technology? Can new forms of remuneration be found to encourage the unemployed to rescue the environment? Can layabouts be put to work caring for the increasing numbers of elderly people at less than the cost of a traditional public sector wage? Or would it be better to adopt an individualistic approach, involving oneself (say) in a multi-million dollar swindle to sell counterfeit money? Fortunately I was diverted from these weighty conundrums by a piece of good news. Cholera in Somalia had killed 675 people between February and June 1994, the United Nations reported. I quietly chuckled at my good fortune. So old yet so alive! Better still, very much better still, the year's toll of infectious diseases. Perks us up no end. Here, in The Dump. Here in this despised recess. Feeding on the scraps of others. Devouring their leavings. Ho! What's this? *A well-regulated militia* comma. *Being necessary to the security of a free state* comma. *The right of the people to keep and bear arms* comma. *Shall not* – CRACK! – *be infringed* – CRACK! Full stop. Tuning in, full stop. To sweet Dolores, full stop. Singing "I Just Shot John Lennon", full stop. To maugre winter's cold and the summer's worst excess. With an anacreontic swagger, no less. More cheering news! The British Housebuilder of the Year Awards were presented during an awards luncheon at the Hilton. Buyers were asked to judge their housebuilder on eleven key areas of customer service. God bless! Ah, the pleasure of porches. How do YOU shelter from the sun? Australians use verandahs and Greeks attach shutters to windows to keep their homes cool. In Britain we have the humble porch. The word porch (from the Latin word porticus) is the entrance area to a home. It not only acts as a shelter from the weather but is a convenient place to store umbrellas, overcoats, shopping bags. The porch is often lit, providing extra security for the householder when he returns home in the evening. Most importantly of all, it provides visitors with their first impression of a home and is a perfect place to hang plants. Or why not enliven your home with a reproduction? Incidentally, did I mention how erratic the news is? Drifts of old newspapers form in The Dump like dirty snow. Like dirty sand dunes. Dirtier even than the dogshitdotted dunes at Hunstanton, proud England's cleanest filthy beach. A story no sooner appears than it vanishes under the drift of a new story. Like the ancient WW2 anti-tank blocks at Hayling, submerged by fresh formations of sand. Elections, for example. Local elections, county council elections, general elections. Immense excitement. No one, of course, votes, but the results are always awaited with keen excitement. The electoral status of the inhabitants of The Dump is something of a puzzle. In theory everyone still has a vote in their old abode, but in practice since no one is able to get back there it is impossible to vote. This does not stop the parties occasionally drifting overhead in hot air balloons. The Conservatives warn ominously of the nightmarish future under a Labour Government. Taxes and prices would rocket. Hordes of discoloured immigrants and glistening aliens would pour in from all quarters of the planet, copulating like rabbits and defecating on posters of Constable's immortal "Haywain". The Labour candidates gaze down from a vast height with a shiny look of immense sympathy for our plight. They assure us that if they ever get elected they will certainly do something about the disgraceful housing to be found in The Dump. Under Labour things will certainly get better, though it is a question of waiting to see how this will happen, it would be unwise to make rash spending commitments. New cardboard roofing is certainly a possibility, though it will not be possible to be sure of this within the lifetime of a single Labour Government. Leo said bitterly that pink balloons had been drifting over The Dump throughout the whole of the twentieth century and nothing had changed. He was hushed to silence by Leopold, who was pointing excitedly at a yellow aerostat. "Look!" he cried excitedly. "Hot Air Liberal Democrats!" Words plummeted down upon us. "Liberals believe in the three ems: in middles, in moderation, in mildness." It began to rain. Someone enquired about the history of The Dump. Traces remain. Bones, possibly of mammoths. Buckets. Old pipe stems. Bits of red brick. Mysterious black pipes. Old signs. LUNATICS ONLY BEYOND THIS POINT and BEWARE. Rusty vats. Bars. Dirty straitjackets. Megaphones. Lengths of flex. Cracked lenses the size of dinnerplates. Coils of bleached film with torn sprockets. It was not far from the mysterious black pipes that I first encountered the literary critic one autumn afternoon. He was sitting on a Michelin tyre, with a disconsolate expression upon his face. Greying, going bald on top, he was a little bearded man in his forties. From the absence of soot and stains on his jacket and trousers I deduced he was a new arrival. Also, his teeth were white and in excellent condition. Good teeth are a dead giveaway. Anyone who has been in The Dump for any length of time inevitably displays a mouthful of rotten teeth, the result of poor diet and a complete absence of dental practitioners. When he saw me he gave a nervous start, and yelped, "How squalid, commonplace and unliterary this whole place is." Then he burst into tears. I allowed him to lean on my shoulder and gave him an encouraging pat on the head. Sobbing, he muttered a peculiar jargon, asking for the direction of the nearest seminar group. He didn't care what period. Normally he was an Eighteenth-Century man (although he did sometimes teach a course on Hemingway), but in the circumstances he was prepared to partake in a discussion of absolutely anything – Silver Poets of the Sixteenth Century, the novels of George Eliot, imagery in Woolf. He was so desperate that he was even prepared to talk about critical theory, something which, as a traditional English empiricist, he abhorred. I shook my head and broke the news that critical seminars did not exist in The Dump. Not wishing to encourage false illusions I also bluntly told him about The Great Barrier. He snorted and gave a rasping laugh. "Your Barrier doesn't bother me," he said. "Critical penetration, that's all that's needed." He set off at once in search of an abandoned copy of *The Principles of Literary Criticism*. I did not see him again until several days later, when I strolled over to The Great Barrier to see how he was getting on. I must admit I was not at all surprised to find him sitting, motionless, on a broken sofa. He was trembling and seemed wet. And his face! A dirty, unwashed, unshaven face. Red-eyed, in fact. In utter misery. All around him lay torn pages of literary criticism. His clothes were filthy and torn. Dirt smeared his elbows, which protruded through the rags. "On Margate Sands," he muttered. Over and over again. "Oh en em ess." Months later was observed waving a cutting. "Where, in Trollope," he screamed, "are the millions who filled the factories worked the mines fought the wars and so created but never shared in the wealth that enabled his characters to rub along so comfortably?" *Michael Hutton, SE5*. A very good question. But such little dramas are rare. Most days nothing happens at all. The occasional blackened banana skin is discovered, is greedily joobled and slanked. Sometimes a brittle crust, perhaps even encrusted with flaked wheat and sesame seeds. An original, unforgettable taste from a far-off land, a remote region of Russia. A loaf made from an original fifth-century recipe, including emulsifiers (E471, E472e), Flour Treatment Agent, Ascorbic Acid and genetically engineered soya beans. But most days neither skin nor crust. Most days you have to get by with a munched mouthful of empty matchbox, or a box of grass cuttings. Most days it just rains ceaselessly and you have to huddle somewhere dry and cosy, as best you can, and starve. And when I say it rains I do not mean a dramatic rain, clattering like pistol shots on old sheets of corrugated iron, backed up by incandescent twigs of lightning, flashes, stupefying thunderclaps, nonsense like that. No. I mean a soft enfeebled rain, barely more than drizzle, the most boring rain imaginable. The sort of rain that makes you want to scoop a shallow grave in the sludge and lie down forever. The sort of rain that makes you think of Berryman, of the Orwell Bridge outside Ipswich. A passing barque. The road to Pin Mill. The cobbled concrete islands upon which the legs of the bridge rest. Some days it doesn't even rain, there's just cloud, grey unending cloud, and nothing happens, not even the rats are out. Some days you have to invent yourself anew. Spent and frail as you are. Do not think I am unaware of the comparison which has been made between myself and Mr Muddle, that popular children's cartoon character who goes through life walking backwards and is forever banging into things, all the while grinning stupidly. Some days you have to make do with licking the rust-coloured sauce left in someone's discarded tin of baked beans. Some days you're so starved and wet and depressed you think you can't face another day, and you start looking at the knife-sharp edge of the tin lid with unspeakable longing. Most days are like this in The Dump. Don't be fooled into thinking life on The Dump is one long round of picaresque adventure. It isn't. My real adventures finished long ago, before I got here. Most days in The Dump are wet and dirty and boring and at best dangerous. But mustn't grumble. Far away in Thailand the 200,000 child prostitutes are going about their business with American sailors and tourists from Japan, France, Germany, the Netherlands and Britain. Far off in Mesopotamia, thousands of slightly under-nourished children not-yet-five are quenching their thirst with brown water. On Smokey Mountain, in Manila, the feverish children scavenge and cough and spit in the ashen rain. After six hours of sorting through garbage for pieces of glass, tin and plastic you can make fifty pesos. What's that? The light's bad over here. My voice is going. Why don't we just trade stories? As Richard Gere says in *Intersection*. Half-senseless sense of an ending. *Dear Sir, I am in a Mad house and quite forget your Name or who you are you must excuse me for I have nothing to communicate or tell of and why I am shut up I don't know I have nothing to say so I conclude.* Once full of youth, radiance, enthusiasms! We shall weather these dreary times yet & drink our bottle together of an evening. Then back to abandonment and rain. Back to the old beginnings. Slime, blood, cord, scissors, scream. Weighing scales. Breast, nipple, slurp. The first howlings. Welcome to the rain. Many of the graves contained personnel items. Welcome to the lands of things that don't work anymore. The rejected, the worthless. The unwanted pages, the unwanted words. Place of desolation. The breakage and the waste. All that's used-up, finished with, gone. Rubbish everywhere. Talk about the environs of Fort Dimanche! A faint amber blotch on the smoky horizon indicating where the dawn sun is beginning its slow, wounded crawl across the grey polluted sky. Of course, it might not have been the sun at all. It might just have been the glow of flames from burning underground tyres. But on that particular morning I was in a good mood. As far as I was concerned it *was* the sun. It seemed to cast a warm, friendly glow over The Dump, turning the rust-powdered burned-out shell of a distant Volkswagen Beetle to burnished gold. It transformed puddles of oil to shimmering rainbow-coloured windows into a world of infinite mystery and beauty. My humble dribble of urine became a noble, bronze arc of the sort triumphant centurions might once have marched beneath. I gazed in delight and wonder as it dropped to mother earth, a triumph of liquid engineering. It splattered loudly across a colourless, rather washed-out portrait of John Major. For some reason – who was he? (the name was obviously bogus) – pictures of this man littered a patch of The Dump, like the object of a personality cult the morning after a people's revolution. The patch was not much of a patch. I remember I was trapped there for a while, as in a mire, my ankles immersed in a foul, sucking ooze. I used to call him the man with the frozen smile. From his phoney "Mr Average" appearance I assumed he was an actor who had fronted an advertising campaign for a major building society, a campaign designed to persuade investors to put their money into an exciting five-star ten-year saving scheme which would allow them to buy that long-longed-for dream house/dream car/world cruise for two but which had flopped miserably, resulting in a mass discarding of publicity material. "Busy old fool, unruly sun, why dost thou thus, through windows, and through curtains call on us?" I playfully bellowed as I zipped up my fly, causing a nearby family of five black mice feasting on the head of an old woman to scamper away in fear. I picked up my binoculars and set off once more across The Dump. I hadn't been walking for much more than an hour when something caught my eye in the distance. The black outline of a human figure, performing a strange ritual by a sack of rubbish. The sack of rubbish was vertical. It was a little like one of those strange packages you see in the warehouse in *Reservoir Dogs*, but darker. Except (tee hee!) it's not a warehouse. I trudged closer. The figure was Welsh, or perhaps Afro-Caribbean. I realised at once what was happening. The man was a fiery socialist who had slithered almost to the top of New Labour. He'd been made a Privy Councillor and hadn't broken the habit. The bloated, foul-smelling sack was obviously intended to be the sovereign. The fiery socialist bowed, and approached the sack. He lowered his right kneecap on to a bucket. He then moved to a second bucket. The buckets were blue and smeared with a brown substance. A limp, rolled, rain-sodden copy of *The Financial Times* protruded from a split in the gross, noxious, gassy sack. The fiery socialist took hold of the pink paper and inserted it into his mouth, chewing on it with anxious, agitated eyes. The sack seemed to shudder, and the newspaper exuded a kind of snotty slime, which the fiery socialist swallowed. Then, without wiping his lips, he stood up and backed away from the sack, his gait spavined, his demeanour fawning, his whole manner something between that of a groggy crab and a kind of sly, bloodshot cockroach. Prescott was his name, sometimes Boateng. Still backing away, he tripped over the second bucket and fell rump-first into an emerald pool, which exploded with a massive, screeching fart. Grinning, Prescott bowed solemnly at the erect sack and returned to repeat the ritual. I passed hurriedly on. I hadn't been walking for much more than an hour when something caught my eye in the distance. Whatever it was was irregular and low on the horizon. In The Dump I had intermittently encountered the outline of things new and strange, but never quite like this. I at once dropped to the ground like a well-trained infantryman and lay flat on my stomach among a pile of dying forsythia branches (you are not supposed to leave out garden refuse for the dustmen, but people do). I raised the binoculars to my eyes and brought the mysterious structure closer. Horrors! The lumps were people's heads. At first glance it looked like a bad case of decapitation, but then to my relief I saw that the heads were moving. There were seventeen of them (twelve men and five women) and they were sitting astride a fence, in a line, as if on an extended version of one of those iron horses you sometimes see in park playgrounds. Their bodies were absolutely motionless, apart from their heads, which were in constant motion, swivelling first one way, then another. I sharpened the focus and examined them carefully. The fence was a stout wooden affair, very reminiscent of the famous picket fence in Dallas, Texas. The fenceposts narrowed at the top to an arrow point and why anyone should want to sit on them seemed baffling. The fence looked very uncomfortable, an impression reinforced by the rather agonized expression on the faces of the sitters. What was particularly striking was the apparent paralysis of the bodies of these people. Their right legs tightly gripped the side of the fence, their right arms were stretched out rigidly and their hands clutched the fencepost immediately ahead of them. Beneath each of them a wooden arrow point embedded itself between the curves of their buttocks. They were facing right, north westward, in the direction of Stratford-upon-Avon and the Isle of Man. But in sharp contrast to the total immobility of their bodies the heads of these people continued to move from side to side in an oddly predictable, mechanical way. They were alive, but what they were up to was anyone's guess. I decided they must be members of some outlandish religious sect, one of the sort that believed in harrowing the flesh and in lengthy periods of meditation. I had never come across a religious cult in The Dump before, but I had heard vague and sinister rumours, and I decided to steer well clear of the folk up ahead of me. They seemed to be quite smartly dressed (through the binoculars I could make out uncrumpled jackets and blue-striped Marks and Spencer shirts) but it was best to be on the safe side. I changed direction ninety degrees and began crawling towards Ypres. I must have crawled for about two miles before I felt it was safe to stand up again. As crawls go it was not a particularly memorable one. I crawled across patches of broken plaster, I crawled through a swathe of soot (messy, nasty stuff), I crawled past blackened, shattered chandeliers, enigmatic amongst empty cement sacks. I crawled past charred remnants of mosaic tiles and a Campbell's soup tin. I came across what might have been a chemical warfare suit, cut to ribbons, useless. I encountered dried excreta, pieces of bone (possibly human), stained Mills & Boon romances with nurses on the cover. At one point I came across an almost empty jar of strawberry jam and paused to lick it clean. I also found the remains of a child's birthday party, and eagerly packed into a brown paper bag a nice collection of broken biscuits, half-eaten cake and nibbled cheese. It was going to be a treat for later. Unfortunately this reeking bag of treasures simply attracted a cloud of flies which absolutely refused to be shooed away. There was nothing for it but to eat it all up there and then. Munching my way through jigsaw-shaped pieces of wheatmeal digestive and lumps of angel cake evoked a familiar feeling in me. I felt like – eh? – the ghost at the banquet. Or an empty echo. Or a sort of dull oozing afterbirth, grey as dripping sperm, reminiscent of the wallpaper paste at the Earle. Sleek, florid, wealthy men in dinner jackets sat with tanned hollow curvaceous elegant women around dinner tables in Knightsbridge and Kensington, not knowing that their little celebration would find an echo a week later in The Dump as a pair of Swillers squatted around the Cordon Bleu scraps on an upturned banana box, passing the greasy leftovers to their ragged, filthy, blistered, companionable whores. Businessmen pushed aside their plate of mousse of sole garnished with salmon, not seeing the filthy trembling hands waiting in the shadows to scoop up the uneaten debris of their greed. Small paper-hatted children spilt crumbs, knocked over fizzy drinks, farted and shrieked and sobbed with birthday fury, oblivious of the wretches lying on a patch of far-off sludge who would greedily devour the tasty morsels of marzipan, the crumpled lump of sponge cake topped with a curl of snot. I sometimes wonder if it isn't the case that every mealtime among the Barbarians gives birth to a repeat performance in The Dump. I remembered what somebody had once said about history repeating itself the first time as drudgery, the second time as farts. Overwhelmed by emotion (and stuffed full of angel cake) I rolled over on to my back and went to sleep. I awoke, aching in every bone. Merde! Les deux fesses dans l'eau, et gelées. Plus each delicate pore of my dappled skin plugged with dirt and icy slime. With trembling fingers I made use once more of the binos. The people on the fence were still there. Plus in exactly the same positions. Their heads continued to swivel from side to side, as if manipulated by an unseen puppeteer. I stood up. I began to cough. The Dump's effluvium was no worse, no better. My throat hurt. I sneezed, once, twice. A shudder ran through my body but soon became tired and started to limp. I farted four brief bursts. Trumpet-like, it was said. Orchestral. Possibly reminiscent of Mozart. It was cold, very cold. I groped about in my shreds and eventually located my wrinkled, petite member. Pointing the barrel at the parliamentary page of a prone broadsheet I waited, grim-faced. After seventeen minutes thirty-seven seconds my pitiful penis finally expelled a pitter-patter of greenish drips. They missed the newspaper and splattered my socks. Brushing drifts of yellow and pink crumbs from my lapels, humming "Kozmic Blues", I continued on towards Ypres. With luck, and assuming I could find a gap in The Great Barrier, and provided I had the strength to swim the English Channel, I estimated I should be in Belgium in ten days' time, knowing full well, of course, that the likelihood of this happening was precisely zero. I walked on. Ahead of me was a low rise of waste paper. I could see bundles of old newspapers and brown sacks split at the sides, spilling documents, important-looking sheets of A4, discarded envelopes, carbon paper, computer listings paper with the perforated strips still attached. The philatelist in me wanted to linger and collect the stamps, but time was getting on and I wanted to see what lay the other side of that papery ridge so reminiscent of Senlac. When I reached the top and saw what was in front of me I gave a low whistle of surprise. No, I tell a lie. I didn't give any sort of whistle, even though it was one of those situations where in the better sort of narrative a low whistle of surprise would not only be called for but would be vigorously indulged in. I am afraid I merely gave a sort of arthritic gasp, at best, and perhaps not even that, never having been a very expressive person. Hearty backslapping, loud whoops and eager embraces are frankly not my cup of tea. Though almost certainly mute, and blank of expression, I was nevertheless amazed at what was there, about six-hundred metres away, on a fairly typical dump plateau of waste. It was enormous and I recognised it at once. It was an American B52 bomber. Its shape, size, grandeur, engine cowlings and enormous wing-span were unmistakeable. I had once made one with an Airfix kit, and I'd sometimes seen the real thing on the telly, so I was quite certain it was a B52. For a moment I thought it had only just crashed, and I felt an immense surge of excitement. All I had to do was run across to the bomber, provide what help I could to the crew, perhaps even try out a spot of first aid, and be airlifted back with them when the Barrier-breaching U.S. army helicopters came to the rescue. The crew would be friendly, gum-chewing blue-eyed young men with crew cuts, named Hank, Chuck, Ron, Johnny, Cary, Jack, Tom and Bob. They would be forever in my debt for having extinguished the flames which threatened the fuel tanks. I would marry Cary's sister Lola, spending my later years in California running a successful pest-extermination agency. The side of the B52 had been torn away and I could see frenzied movement inside. I was about to charge down the far side of the low hill, ankle deep in white ash, a sour, urgent look on my face, when something made me pause. Something was not quite right. For a start, if the bomber had just crashed, why hadn't I seen or heard it come down? I sank down to the ground and concealed myself behind a large cardboard box. I adjusted the binoculars and scanned the aircraft. There were people inside the fuselage of the aircraft, and the aircraft looked as if it had crashed (why? when?). But it had obviously crashed a long time ago. It was an adapted B52 I was looking at. The vast interior of the aircraft had been divided up into what were unmistakably committee rooms, each of which contained a committee table and some committee members. In each committee room there were six people vigorously nodding their heads, and another six people emphatically shaking theirs. The committee members were dressed in light casual clothes and were strikingly reminiscent of the strange people astride the picket fence. At the front of the B52 an area had been set aside for worship. An enormous stars and stripes hung from the ceiling to the floor, and a group of worshippers could be seen before it, prostrate on a deep-pile carpet. I scanned the area around the bomber, and observed that there were a number of other fences dotted around, each of which had its quota of familiar sitters. Everywhere I looked heads were turning from side to side as if propelled by little wind machines. Although the total population of The Dump probably runs into hundreds (even thousands) (even, some would say, tens of thousands) I had never encountered so many people together in the same place. I felt a little glow in my heart. I had, at long last, come across a community! It was like being present at the beginnings of a society. One day there would be houses here, car parks and a church, a litle shop on the corner selling milk, yogurt and laxatives. One day there would be a school, an ambulance station, a police station, a barracks, an art gallery, a bookshop, a biological weapons research centre. It was too exciting for words – so I said nothing. Baffled by the strange activities in and around the B52, I shifted my attention to the far side of the great aircraft. Beyond the smooth navy-blue nosecone could be seen one of the B52's immense, slug-shaped 500lb bombs. It rested on the ground, wedged firm by two of its tail fins. A young man was lying on his stomach on the bomb, and a line of other young men were queueing patiently, awaiting their turn. At first I thought the man on the bomb was doing press-ups, and it was only when the to and fro motions of his upper thighs and rear reached a sudden frenzy that I at last understood. There were some other unpleasant surprises. Scanning the area at the back of the B52, I encountered a vast cratered wasteland dotted with overlapping circles of stagnant water. The ground was churned-up and slushy and littered with splintered, unidentifiable metallic wreckage. There were also scatterings of bone and several broken black sacks which were not black sacks at all. There was a stench of chicken soup and diarrhoea. Bits of bone were everywhere – leg bones, arm bones, lumbar vertebrae, innumerable rib-cages, smashed skulls, sphenoids, broken bits of pelvis, lengths of clavicle. I moved back to re-examine the bomber. As I did so I spotted something I'd missed. Something that was going on towards the rear of the aircraft. A solid iron hook had been attached to the underside of the fuselage and a primitive pulley system had been set up. Another of the 500lb bombs had been winched up on a chain by its tail fins, and hung in the air, nose downward. The chain was moved by a small steering wheel, evidently cannibalised from an abandoned car. The nose of the bomb was of a dark purple colour, edged by splashes of bright red. Why this was became evident a moment or so later. I suddenly saw that at the back of the plane, underneath the tail, was a cage. It was made out of wood and held half a dozen small, dark figures I recognised as Underdogs. The Underdogs were squealing and sobbing, and even at that distance I could hear their little shrieks of anxiety. I was not surprised, since Underdogs have such a strong aversion to daylight. Even as I watched, some young men in strawberry pink blazers clambered up on top of the cage, opened a hatchway, reached in, and dragged out an Underdog. The Underdog kicked and bit, until subdued with truncheons. Then they dragged him (I think it was a him) to what appeared to be a purple slab. Here they forced the Underdog on his back on to the slab and attached chains to his arms and legs. The slab was directly underneath the winched bomb. One of the pink-blazered men began to turn the wheel. The nosecone of the bomb trembled, swung a little from side to side, then steadied and began slowly to descend. The Underdog, eyes swelling like plums, began to writhe. And then it happened. As if from nowhere Underdogs emerged from all sides and swarmed towards the inhabitants of the B52. They came from behind rubbish sacks, out of cardboard boxes, from behind burned-out cars. They emerged like the dead from the bowels of the earth. There were scores of them, hundreds of them. I was astonished by their vigour and unity. In the past I had only ever seen them cowering in ditches, or peeking out from barrels. Underdogs are passive, shy, subservient, cowed, feeble, ingratiating, humble, cowardly, grateful-for-small-mercies and above all solitary and isolated. Yet here they were, on the attack, like an army! I swung the binoculars from side to side, astonished by what I was witnessing. The young men in pink blazers seemed stupefied by what was happening. They stood statuesque and motionless, as if dipped in liquid helium, mouths gaping open. A crowd of Underdogs swarmed over them, chopping them down. The man with his hand on the wheel fell forwards, both hands pressed against his stomach. From between his fingers protruded a black arrow. Someone torched the bomber. Flames began to lap the cockpit. The stars and stripes erupted in fire, showering the worshippers in sparks. Shrieks and screams carried in the still air. Now the tail was also spewing smoke. The Underdogs backed away as the fire took hold. Almost as quickly as they had appeared they were gone, swarming back into holes in the earth, disappearing into the elaborate network of subterranean tunnels and bunkers where they live and work. Suddenly there was an immense, shattering explosion. It was followed almost immediately by a second thunderclap of noise. A pillar of white light surged into the sky, sending out boiling black clouds in every direction. The force of the explosion catapulted me backwards down the slope, where by great good fortune my fall was cushioned by a mattress. I lay there, winded. Then a more powerful force threw me into reverse. I flew back up the slope, landing on my feet. The billowing smoke shrank and was sucked away, the fragments of bomber miraculously collided and formed a seamless whole. The cast of my preposterous drama ran jerkily backwards, hither and thither, like scalded ants. I myself moved backwards, gasping like a fish, nausea slopping around in my guts, a dark streak flashing across my vision as it yielded a glimpse of the hands of my wristwatch performing dizzy backward rolls. In next to no time I found myself back on top of that papery ridge, observing instead of a B52 a vast wilderness of rubbish, into the portals of which I vomited, colourfully. It started to rain. Rain always makes me think of the time I wasn't crushed and drowned by the great mill wheel. I dived to the bottom of the racing stream and swiftly located a length of rusted tubing. I used it to breathe through until the stupid police had gone. The chance discovery of the mangled cadaver of a tramp satiated their turgid desire for D following on from C. I was present at my own funeral, chuckling delightedly as I peeked through the shrubbery. I have visited my banal, unmarked grave on many subsequent occasions, marvelling at the spring in my gait. Walter Grannage, a murderer! The very idea. I may be a little demented. I may have turned my living room into a shrine to M. I may have been over-fond of kisses from little Judy. I may have many quirks (rubbing my hands, waltzing, babbling on about the past). But the idea that I slipped away from *Tristan und Isolde* in order to waggle the ladder on which my poor wife stood, toppling her into the greenhouse and severing her jugular! Who, then? Who slipped arsenic into that bedtime milk? I should have thought that was obvious. Scrutiny of Doctor Boswell's medical qualifications might be a starting point. The name is surely bogus, eh, Inspector Johnson? An interview with the pregnant girl he abandoned in that boarding house in Bournemouth might yield insights into his devious character, his propensity to violence, his interest in poisons and his bizarre sexual appetites. Or how about putting Nurse Marlow into a cold, unfurnished cell for forty-eight hours and breaking that fiery spirit of hers. A slippery, lying slut if ever I saw one. Talk about Lady Macbeth! Perhaps she put them both up to it. Evenbridge reeks. Yes, reeks. Behind those long drives and lace curtains. Your mind would boggle if you knew. Pornography, silver needles, strange and unnatural practices. Complete editions of the Marquis de Sade and Winston Churchill. Framed signed photographs of Margaret Thatcher. Whips. Pickles. And do not overlook Judy. A snickering little Lolita if ever there was one. Seriously disturbed. The things she knew. Eggs. Parsnips. The tricks she got up to with the grown-ups. Your mind would boggle if you knew. They were all in it. Just like *The Stepford Wives*. All except poor M. That was why they had to get rid of her. Once she found out. The strain of trying to keep up appearances. Wondering who to turn to. Telling the police. A big mistake, that. She didn't know the leader of the coven was Chief Superintendent Blair. A weasel-eyed bi-sexual goat-worshipping pederast if ever there was one. You only had to be in the same room as him to sense the evil in him. Poor M. She told me everything. About Judy. About Welling. About her desperate quest for an orgasm (clitoral or vaginal, she really didn't mind). "Come with me," I said. "My love, my dearest. My little alligator." And she came. And came. And came again. And they found out. And that is why I languish here, in the old, derelict mill, my house empty, unsold. I am old and bald and confused. My bones ache. Soon I will have no alternative but to gather up my scraps, my darling darling's scraps and knick-knacks and the knickers with the exciting stains. I'll slip them into my old battered suitcase. And slip away. Away down the slippery road to the railway station. I think I may slither to Vienna and waltz, waltz, waltz away the icy night. Sorry. The gears in my mind are slipping. My mind is wandering. Oh my railway spine! The rain came harder, faster. My thoughts turned briefly to the Newport rising. The thought of my impotence was bitter. Angrily I reached for my poor old turkey-necked pecker. I tugged back the foreskin, knocked away a crust of purple fungus and squashed a handful of the tiny crunchy creatures which thrived in the hot mildew of my raw flesh. At once I felt better. I buttoned up my bonnet, tightened my scarf. From my tucker bag I removed my pocket atlas and stared at the pages. Ust Labinsk! Vatomandry! Vijayadurg! Yaapeet. Xau and Zell and Zvonce. So many places I would never get to, not now. Trapped as I am in The Dump. But mustn't grumble. Such is life. An endless passage between a snore and a fart. No hope now of ever exploring the environs of Whitby, say, or Irbid. But mustn't grumble. Goodbye, Tongue. No chance of going with Callinicos up the Caicos Passage. No use now for that toy compass, its little palsied silver needle throbbing with uncertainty. No risk of being tempted by fraud on Crooked Island. Staring at the precipitation graph for Ilfracombe I began to wonder where my old friend Bones might be. On the Rue du Jour, peut-être? Claremont Road? He might be anywhere. I closed the book, re-opened it at random and saw that my forefinger was resting on Peru. "Merde," said the clocharde, beginning the complicated task of getting up. I therefore set off in that direction. I thought to myself, self number eighteen, I thought: be in good heart! Goodheart? Lionheart? My baffled heart. My paper heart. Arthur Cravan! My cold, cold heart. Cheer up! This bright day is different to all the others! Polly unpopped her pillbox packed with pink powder, patted it upon her parrot. The parrot let out a satisfied, wicked laugh. "Eh?" screeched self nineteen. "You wanna watch *Track 29*." "Reality or nothing!" "Friends, comrades, countrymen!" interjected a voice, stronger and louder than all the others. A fruity voice, almost certainly going by the name William, although the case has been put for John, Joan and Wolfgang. "This sweet day," cried the voice, "is the day I let go of my tale." As the mad dog said to the actress. Tale? Aha! A goodly narrative. An accurate rendering of the noises that human beings currently make in their daily simple needs of communication. I have written it all down, yes. I, furious Ronald, cycling furiously – no! recycling furfuraceously – I have done my very best. Half-deranged? You bastard! Why not a quarter? Why not three-quarters? Eighty-five per cent. Eh? No matter. Get lost, you beast! Hope you wind up in The Dump. A real jungle. Plenty of time here to speculate about a possible echo of Hawthorne's garden of death, eh? To consider the cruellest month. To fill in your wilderness days with a wild memoir. But no foulness; no phonological couplings. No homophones, thank you very much! The compositors bugger it up for you in the end, of course. Printing prose as verse and verse as prose, anything to stretch that prick and swell that void. F into Q2? Don't fucking make me laugh! A paraphrase will contribute to everyone's understanding. Sick Malc, say. In the dark tavern. Which is bitter. Zip Koade. Cromer Switchman. Henri Looney. Bucky Binns. Tiny O'Toole, swollen with lust. Hear that? "Read me selections from the Bodleian MS. Laud Misc. 581!" The voice sounded tired, shaky. Hungarian. American, almost. It began to croon a Steve Earle number, "Billy Austin" by the sound of it. Broke off, and in a Wenatchee accent whispered, movingly, "Mais où sont les neiges d'antan?" Bloody shut up harping on about the past! cried Aeolian, breaking wind. The voice ceased on the midnight hour, began yanking out a memory. "Gook tries to put the fire out while you're trying to burn his hootch, he fucks with you, you fuck with him, right? You push him away, or kick his ass, or you do what we usually did which was to shoot him. You can't see anything because of the smoke. Awful smell. All kinds of shit burning. Bodies all over the place. Near me was a dead old woman holding a spattered copy of *The Ambassadors*. And a young girl. She'd lost one leg and was going round in a circle on the ground, crying out 'Why? Why is that in Jane Austen we sit quite resigned in an arrested spring?' A marine flipped her over, pummelled her walnut, stuck it in, grunted, shot his load. Erect above all for her was the sharp-edged fact of the relation of the whole group, individually and collectively, to herself – herself so speciously eliminated. Yes, took out he afterwards the marine a handgun and shot dripping her in the head. I was completely pissed by the fucking thing, all of it. All I wanted to do was trash people and that's what I did." A marbled, iridescent text. With many recognitions. Bleak solo cello, a woodwind's cry. That Finn again! Suppose that instead of a biped upon a stage concealing and betraying his thought we watch the thought itself, the hidden thing, as it twists to and fro, fro and two and three. Ah, how sweet it is to grasp the shadowy and phantasmal form of a book, to stroke its spine and kiss its delicate chapters. To turn it over and plunge in and frown and grunt and sweat. This whole world is a copy of some of the bits from another, the more normal world! The deviations open to Flaubert are innumerable! Doesn't have to be a book of course. Something shorter would do. Pamphlets seditious, profane, scandalous rebellious, Atheisticall, and Blasphemous (besides nonsensicall the most grievous of all). And afterwards? How sweet it would be to win The Governor General's Award! Or The Inspector General's. Or a General Inspection. Or to provoke a stormy General Synopsis. To assist the mentally impaired with useful questions enabling them to master any exam, for example: *Hardy was always interested in music. What evidence is there in Hardy's poetry that he preferred Fleetwood Mac to Nico?* To be applauded for my compulsive readability, my style and verve. To become useful to the State. To campaign for the reinstatement and extension of decree number 02030 (1968) of the Central Committee of the Communist Party of the Soviet Union. Be rewarded with truffles, cars, pianos, etc. To be able to drop a line to Celia Kirwan of the Information Research Department. *Dear Celia, I haven't written earlier because I have really been rather poorly. I could, if it is of any value, give you a list of journalists and writers who in my opinion are crypto-communists, fellow-travellers or inclined that way.* Ah, to be a writer! To fondle and tickle and chew and wiggle and ejaculate words! To risk the wrath of the New York Court of Special Sessions! To have relations with publishers! To drop a note (May 28, 1859) to Franz Duncker in Berlin or – more recently – to S. Assersohn in London. To submit and wait. And wait. And wait. *I am sending you today under separate cover a manuscript entitled "Orpheus and Other Poems." Enclosed find postage for its return if the manuscript be not accepted.* To foam, to be rabid! To triumph, alone. To tear it, language, with teeth and paws, ravenously! Savagely! Synapses uncoordinated, connectives misdirected, linkages lost in excesses of verbiage! Gorgeous! Devastating rather than creating! Ah, for the sansculottism of eloquence! The oratory of a Silenus drunk with anger only! To be ragged and rapid, strong and rough, yet neologistic, expressionistic, often incantatory and hypnotic! *The Beneficent Spider* would be a good title I have always thought. To be a writer, yes! Jones and the other man carried the coffin up the stairs. To knock together something full of political animus, sensual liveliness, English and popular instincts! Coarse, elementary, swarming with ignoble vermin, like that which appears in a great decomposing body! Learning how to gasp and convulse amid a surge of the shorter early Saxon verbs! To note *Last year I wrote 282,100 words, exclusive of rewriting. I made no particular advance commercially. I had several grave disappointments.* Un pisseur de copie! Exulting in exquisite moments of syntactical uncertainty! To be not afraid to speak out, no. *There is a need for a firm even implacable theoretical and political fight against the petty-bourgeois tendencies of the opposition, an implacable ideological fight which should go parallel with very cautious and wise organisational tactics. Be extremely firm but don't lose your nerve! P.S. The evils come from (i) bad composition (ii) lack of experience.* I shall show every respect for the proprieties, naturally. Grammar, syntax. Besides endeavouring to curb my fondness for conditional clauses. Only trimming polysyllables where absolutely necessary. Cutting verbs and participles only where superfluous. Chapters. The chapter of landscapes. Hills, sir, and the sundown, and a pink, patched inflatable doll. The chapter of the white cottage. The chapter of false, malicious and factious libel. The chapter beginning: *It is not worth telling, this story of mine – at least, not worth writing.* The chapter of the blister. The chapter of erotic reminiscences. The chapter of the wedding with the adventure of the lost key. The chapter of mountains. The chapter of Shakespeare's missing years. The chapter beginning: *"You are a lovely man, Gussy, but I wish you were a woman,"* *big Alois said facetiously when he had squeezed me into the hole.* The chapter ending: *I put two biscuits by his bed in case he woke and turned the light out.* The chapter beginning: *It was after they had gone that he truly felt the difference, which was most to be felt moreover in his faded old rooms.* The chapter ending: *We walked along together all going fast against time.* The chapter of motels. The chapter of London. The chapter of St. Anton. Of Seattle. And Dachau. Of the nervous collapse. Of the melancholy return. Two hundred chapters of madness. The chapter of plagiarisms. The chapter of striking metaphors. (*I had noticed her shudder when the front-door bell pierced the silence as sharply as a serpent's fang breaks the skin. That warm London afternoon saw him jangling like some battered piano in an Alma-Tadema house, the lid open and mad rats gnawing and scraping at the wires. Giant brown cockroaches, the feet zigzagged until they came to a solid stop. A prostitute hailed us, a sound with the sweetness of poisoned orchids in the forest of the sleeping town.*) The chapter of long walks. The chapter of answers. I shall pile them, one on top of the other, until the manuscript is eight metres high and hailed as. As a towering achievement. Reading down through its dense vastness. All the way through to. Its ephemeral "end" hailed. As a truly rewarding task though. Here's a professorial tip for impatient readers who may have bogged down on that. That difficult second page namely go. Straight to page fifty-seven where. Things really begin. To. Crackle or if that still leaves. Too many pages to tackle skip. The chapter of long walks and jump. Straight to the final section, especially the. The last couple of. Pages. The chapter of inexplicable phenomena. And jokes! Elephants, telephone boxes, cogs, turnips, f-stops, beards, actresses, precision screws. Fascinating facts. The Bible contains 3,566,480 letters, 773,746 words and 31,102 verses. DESUDATION: This term is applied when any unusually violent sweating takes place. Are you, perhaps, too warmly clad? Dust your skin at once with a powder consisting of zinc oxide and starch. (See also SWEAT, DISAGREEABLE.) And other useful tips. Out of sorts? Have you tried effleurage? This is a stroking movement which may be done with either one hand, both hands, or the palmar surface of the fingers and thumb. The hand should be moulded to fit the contour of the part being massaged and the movements should be carried out slowly, smoothly, and rhythmically, if a soothing effect is sought. For stimulating effects brisk and firm strokes are recommended. The LOFTIEST ACTIVE VOLCANO is Popocatapetl – "smoking mountain" – thirty-five miles south-west of Puebla, Mexico. Challenging assertions! "The earth goes round the sun?" said Swayne incredulously. His mind was clear and though he looked tired his expression was serene, almost happy, and there was a cheerful, warm glow in his eyes. The proof that this earth moves around the sun lies in the parallax of the stars? Stuff and nonsense! In the last two-thousand years the earth has travelled 819,936,000,000 miles, agreed? Now this distance is four-thousand five-hundred times the distance that is the base line for orbital parallax, right? In that case displacement of the stars by solar-motion parallax in two-thousand years should be four-and-a-half thousand times the displacement by orbital parallax in one year! Give to orbital parallax as minute a quantity as is consistent with the claims made for it and the Great Dipper would be twisted, the Sickle of Leo nicked! But not a star in the heavens has changed more than doubtfully since the stars were catalogued by Hipparchus two thousand years ago! If, then, there ARE minute displacements of stars that are attributed to orbital parallax, THEY WILL HAVE TO BE EXPLAINED IN SOME OTHER WAY. Unless, of course, you wish to subscribe to the DELUSION that the Sun is moving from Sirius towards Vega. In short, contrary to what a foul conspiracy of SCIENTISTS wishes us to believe, the earth is MOTIONLESS. As common sense ought to tell you. Do you REALLY believe you are travelling at 70,000mph on some sort of gigantic, spinning football floating magically in space? I mean, COME OFF IT. Scattered twos put together. Fours stored up in mind to give a good papery yield. The life and adventures of Scriblerus! I was always a putter-inner rather than a taker-outer. The occasional autobiographical tit-bit to whet the appetite of my future biographers. The fag-end of that summer with Monika, with whom I still keep in – *sic* – touch. Her legs had the specialized tension common to aerial workers. But she went away – and the dash should be as long as the earth's orbit. My darling, I have been with Zumps. I have got you a hammer and a pair of pliers to twist your wire with. May every one, my dear, vibrate sweet comfort to my hopes! I had reasons for my behaviour which, if they could not be approved, could yet be discussed. Ton souvenir en moi luit comme un ostensoir! That Saturday afternoon, we lay in bed in one another's arms. After a tumultuous fuck we watched *Star Trek*. The episode in which the starship begins – horrors – to dissolve. Sweating, Scotty wielded his tool. He fingered it deftly, brought the surge of liquefaction to an end. I turned you over. Madam, there's a bite! John called out to me from the hallway. I answered him stiffly. I was afraid he would open the door and come into the room. Moments later (blessed relief) I heard the front door slam. Monika, Monika. To me you will always be as you were then, your dark hair almost down to your waist. You loaned me your precious copy of *Sahaeijueoi Nodongja*. You did not mind that I was in the grip of annotations. Your grasp of the General Law of Capitalist Accumulation was firm, your lips slender and voracious. To me faire friend you never can be old. I shall always remember your muddy complexion and foul vocabulary, your bleary eyes, your dripping nose and oozing gash. The loose slack feel of your skin, your corseted hips, the way you drove down the dew with a pair of heels as broad as two wheels! 'Tis impossible to describe what I have suffered since I saw you last, I am sure I could have bore the rack much better than those killing, killing words of yours. I want you to be aware that I know you have treated me infernally – infernally! There is a great gulph between us. My dear, my darling, do you hear me where you sleep? I live in a bye corner of the kingdom in a vast unfurnished house; my family consists of nowt but a steward, a groom, a helper in the stable, a footman, a diseased Nietzschean and an old maid. I am prone to fits of depression, no getting away from it. Your true friend and Injun Cowboy. PS Section 3 of the 1983 Mental Health Act is naked fascism! All's ill with me now. I live in a constant endeavour to fence against the infirmities of ill health. Deaf, giddy, helpless. My sufferings alleviated by but a daily half pint of wine and some new great tasting corn chips made from fresh flame-grilled corn with twenty-five per cent less fat than potato crisps, in three irresistible flavours: tangy cheese, savoury beef and spicy chicken. It rains every day. People understand me so little that they do not even understand when I complain of being misunderstood. As Kierkegaard remarked. Thank Christ for easy to use, non-leak, non-drip caps. Man that is born of a woman, is of few days, and full of trouble. But nothing revives body and mind like a herbal hair and body gel with a secret blend of 13 herbs and minerals and a revitalising fresh herby fragrance. Even with this gel my life admittedly has not been without its ups and downs. The coughing. The coffin poem. The day I was fitted with my set of false teeth, only the upper okay. The time I bought a hot water bottle. It was made of rubber. In time, it perished. The time I borrowed two shillings and sixpence. A Thursday, it was raining. The fits of coughing were so severe that I had to double up when I coughed. I greeted trains with a howl. The fever tired me a great deal. Sweat broke out on my forehead. My whole body trembled. Round about me only boredom and despair! I could not do without auxiliary constructions, powerful deflections, substitutive satisfactions, intoxicating substances! Oh! W! X! Y! Z! In complete helplessness barely wrote two pages. My career in aroma management never took off. I make ends meet. In fits and starts. I presume the printer has brought you the offspring of my *poetic mania*. Four is good being square! May Jupiter Feretrius grant that I languish not by the Eurotas. *Audi Samuelem.* I occupy myself, eh? Carving figures of birds and beasts out of the turnip parings in my lap. I demand a hearing before the North Thames region mental health review tribunal! I want to get out of here! I want to go shopping! Go shopping, yes. Shopping? I should cocoa! I have bought you ten handsome brass screws, to hang your necessaries upon. I purchased twelve but stole a couple from you to put up in my own cabin. I shall never hang or take my hat off one of them but I shall think of you. And drink of you. And stink of you. Adieu, brat. Feverish? Just a little. Le dérèglement de tous les sens, eh? I am a sick man, I am an angry man. I am an unattractive man. And you? You'll shine more bright in these contents. Ah, language! A voluptuous release. It took – primate brain circuits working overtime – five million years to get here. So, damn you, you might at least pay attention. Thanks. As I was saying. A book. In the agglomerative style. As soon as my work comes out, it will be published in French. A worthy follow-up to *Dictes and Sayinges of the Philosophers* and *Tyranipocrit Discovered* and *Telephone Selling Techniques That Really Work.* And whatnot. To be deposited in all the proper places. Aberystwyth, even. Cydnabyddir yn ddioichgar dderbyn yr eitem hon/eitemau hyn, a anfonwyd yma yn unol â gofynion Deddf Hawlfraint, 1 & 2 Siôr V, pen. 46.15 a SI 1987 No. 918. No sweat!

No go. No go. Land of abandonment and rain. Place of bottles and cast-offs. "Compulsively readable" – *Sunday Express*. "A dazzling postmodernist voyage to the foul, stinking underside of late capitalism" – *Mail on Sunday*. "Anyone who likes a good story will love *The Dump*, which is a wonderful, surprising novel all about friendships and daily life in East London. It is hilarious and moving with a magically happy ending which cheers you up for days afterwards" – *Socialist Review*. "When I first read the book I found the opening movement rather slow and dragging and I believed the final section to be superfluous. I am now convinced that every word is essential, both dramatically and musically" – Jake Berlitz, *The Sun*. *The Dump*, yes. A glorious title. Producers falling over themselves for the movie rights. Starring Mel as Jack and Meryl as Mary. A film of truly epic proportions. Original score by Jarré Junior. *Set out with Mel on an adventure that is both a visual extravaganza and a wry comedy of East End life. Laugh along with Mel at the wonderfully observed scenes of domestic life.* "Can you make the tea, Mary?" "Yes of course I can, Jack. Is there any water in this kettle?" "See for yourself, Mary." "Ah, yes. I can see it now. But where are the teacups?" "The teacups are in the cupboard. Can you find them?" "Yes. Here they are." "Hurry up, Mary! The kettle's boiling." "Piss off Jack and make it yourself, you lazy bugger." "But why, Mary?" "Because I am busy with other things, Jack." "What things, Mary?" "I am pondering the stars, Jack. A hundred thousand million stars, Jack, turning in the circle of the Milky Way. I can never look at them without wondering from which of them the emissaries are coming. A brisk mental interlude from this absorbing account of Dirac's efforts to relate the theory of relativity to the quantum theory." "Well, bugger me." "That's not my cup of tea, Jack. Not even with this handsomely proportioned courgette." "I can't see any courgette, Mary. I can see some spoons, but I can't see any courgette. I can see some hammers, but I can't see any courgette. I can see some cups, but I can't see any courgette. I can see some coffee, but I can't see any courgette." "You need your glasses, Jack." "I suppose so, Mary. Why are you frowning, Mary?" "Because I am concentrating, Jack." "Quantum theory, did you say, Mary?" "I did, Jack, yes.

You see the quantum theory's dung to blauds the classic picture o' the world. You see, Jack, relativity theory can be understood within the framework of classical physics. Events that occur in space and time. But quantum theory challenges the very epistemological foundations of science." "I see, Mary. I think. Mary, what are you doing with that vase?" "I am going to put it on the radio, Jack." "Don't do that. Give it to me." "What are you going to do with it, Jack?" "I am going to put it here in front of the window." "Be careful! Don't drop it! Don't put it there, Jack. Put it here, on this shelf. There we are! It's a lovely vase. It goes nicely with the courgette." "And with the dustjacket of your book on elementary particles, Mary!" "So it does, Jack." "Those flowers are lovely too." "Yes, they are. Yes." "Oh look! It is another fine day today. Mr Jones is with his family." "All his family are diseased, did you know?" "Yes, I did know that, Frank." "They are walking over the bridge, Mary." "The bridge that is about to explode?" Yes, that bridge." "Oh, look. There are some boats on the river. Some horribly burned people are jumping off the boats." "Sally is crouched by the wall. She is doing a big shit. The shit drops into the river. The shit is going under the bridge. The bridge explodes." "Tim is watching the bridge explode." "Tim is diseased, too." "Yes, I know." A lump of débris hits Tim. Tim drops into the burning river. An aeroplane flies over the river. The aeroplane is from the United States of America. It carries an atomic bomb. The aeroplane drops the bomb. The bomb falls. Look at the city! What has happened to it? Where is everyone? "I don't know," said Jack. "Can you make the tea, now, Jane? "Yes, of course I can, Jack. Is there any water in this kettle?" "See for yourself, you bitch." "Where's that tea, dipshit?" "It's over there, you cunt. Behind that fucking teapot. Can't you fucking see it?" "I can see the fucking teapot but I can't see the tea." "There it is! It's there in front of you!" "Ah, yes. I can see it now. But where are the teacups?" Discomfort guides my tongue. Worn out. Blistered. "An elenctic masterpiece; like electro-shock; electrovalent in structure; the ellipses are terrific" – *The Echo*. Thunderous orchestral score, melancholy tortured violins. Don't miss it. *The Dump* has it all: comedy, romance, suspense. With dazzling special effects. No expense has been spared. The odour of human excrement will be pumped into every auditorium to create that extra touch of authenticity. All-star cast. *The Dump* – a spectacular film created from a fascinating story. Admittedly at present nothing much more than a few soiled pages, a scrawl here and there. But one day... I can dream, can't I? Counterfeit an hundred dogged fables, eh? My scraps held in an air-conditioned vault at the Sterling Memorial Library, Yale. My lust for... Sorry, must dash. My blanks and ellipses a matter of continuing scholarly hatreds. One day I shall come to something, eh? You mark my words. One day more than scrawls, much more. A thick wadge of words. Words! Springing from line to line like so many monkeys, pointing, grinning, chattering, howling, biting. Pastiche, parody. The sweetest of allusions. Taking care to avoid gross hanging participles. Vibrant, vigorous vignettes. Venereal texts voided verbatim! A novella, say. Almost a book, perhaps one day to be a real book. A real book! Bliss! Perhaps one day to be translated into Dutch, Peruvian, Martian. Perhaps a Translator's Note at the start. That droll one prefacing *The Sweet Cheat Gone*, for example. A real book, with a spine. A handsome jacket to beat off the dust. Printed on one hundred per cent recycled paper, friendly to whales, using no artifical colours, edible (a boon in a siege). Not merely recycled. Paper which in every way meets the guidelines for permanence and durability of the Committee on Production Guidelines for Book Longevity of the Council on Library Resources. A book with a countdown on the verso, indicating its absolute unpopularity across the lengthening years. 10 9 8 7 6 5 4 3 2 1. A book not afraid to exhibit tributes from impartial admirers. THE BISHOP OF SODOR AND MANN: "What a lot of work you have put into it!" MRS L. COHEN, O.B.E., J.P., Leeds: "I have been arrested and thrilled by the perusal of your book." CHARLES W. HOPPER: "I do not claim to know anything about literature but I read your book with the keenest interest. Congratulations on piloting your Saucy Little Bark into Fame's Eternal Harbour." Herr FITZ J. STARKE, Ph.D., Berlin: "I am writing this from the Bay of Biscay. Your book is nothing less than a joy to me in my seventy-sixth year. It is quite a straight story. It gripped me and instructed me." Thanks. And thanks to the Keeper of Printed Books. Thanks to to the thin, frail, stooped, malnourished figures whose names I could never be bothered to learn, whose risible role in life is to wander, draped in cobwebs, along shadowy aisles, servicing the stacks in the Bodleian. Miss E. C. Lay helped to minimize the difficulties which beset a scholar working away from his home base. My old friend Alison Rump helped me with a number of difficult passages. Thanks to Canada Dry for a much needed tonic. Thanks to everyone involved. Thanks to my nameless typists, whose hysterical female whingeing about Repetitive Strain Injury obliged me to contact the agency, which sacked them on the spot. Ingratiating thanks to my well-heeled in-laws, bearded Rear-Admiral and whiskery Mrs Buttle, who have regularly ruined pleasant Sunday afternoons with their repeated descriptions of how blows from a spring driven electro-magnetically controlled hammer on a steel diaphragm which is in contact with water in a tank secured to the hull produces a sound impulse which is transmitted through the water to the hull of the ship, which acts as a diaphragm, and re-transmits the impulse to the vast fin-filled waters beyond the hull, impulse upon throbbing impulse which, like a continuous rhythmical fart, echoes back from the ocean's arse, three every second, to be received in a hydrophone which is secured to a tank in the same manner as the transmitter, and who have never failed to warn me of the danger of false echoes, Mrs Buttle crooking her finger waggishly, the Rear-Admiral flushed and intense as he bellows that muddy bottoms do not give such good echoes as hard, sandy or rocky bottoms. Thanks to the University of Penge for appointing me as Sesquicentennial Fellow of the Institute for Leisure Studies and Latin American Dancing, without which your amorphous mass of disreputable energies would never have been able to comprehend that foot changes in the Samba are not difficult and are achieved by stepping forward or backward with or without turn, using right or left foot. For gross lack of encouragement I should like to thank my addled Head of Department, Professor Humpbum, for whom Lenin's favourite adjective, cretinous, might well have been exclusively invented.

(Hambone, whose remaindered books I have encountered heaped and dust-coated from Southwold to rainy Goodge Street.) A tale, yes. Destined for publication, no doubt. A worthy successor to my previous international best-sellers *The Albugineous Bouillon* and *Lengthening Trousseaus*. Not to mention my smash-hit self-help collaboration with Mick Dooly, *Engild Viduage*. I have written it all down, yes. I have done my very best. Admittedly much left unsaid, so much undescribed, or quite forgotten, or returning in too late flashes, or rotted away into vaguenesses and mists. The free market ideologues, reduced to eating their own flesh. Not forgetting the aerostat-hater, Hitler. Looked like him, anyway. Same sort of moustache. I met him on a Saturday. He was hunched over a pile of dirty paper, trying to set light to it. Hearing the crunch of footsteps he whirled round, eyes bulging. "Burn them!" he shrieked. "My personal papers! The Bolsheviks must not see them!" The stench was that of excrement and rotting apples. His hair was as lank and floppy as in the photographs. Not so his face, all puffy and discoloured, chin and brow blue with lack of oxygen. His right arm began to tremble violently. He seized it with his left arm and unsuccessfully tried to quieten it down. "Burn them!" Hitler frothed. The froth reminded me of the yellowish scum blown ashore by the strong winds at Brancaster beach. His left leg (God had not failed to observe or forget a single furtive spurt) began to twitch uncontrollably. "Shoot them all, shoot them all!" he frothed afresh. His eyes were Margaret Thatcher's at the retaking of South Georgia. From the pile of unlit paper he snatched a map and bit into it. It was an out-of-date street map of Berlin. The ground shuddered as sudden explosions encircled us. I could hear the crackle of small arms fire. The Russians were only two blocks away. With his left index finger Hitler jabbed at the map, tearing shreds out of it. He called for Panzers but none came. He put on a grotesque rubber Thatcher mask. "Everyone has betrayed me!" he screamed. Distinctly uffish, you might say. I realised with a shock he was addressing yours truly. It was all too much for me. I ran off over a low grassy knoll, brushing aside two C.I.A. men. Such pretty mugwort! But the hill tried to throw me off balance with its wobbles and squirts of foul gas. Buried animal cadavers, I guessed. Herds of diseased cattle and radioactive sheep fled in panic across my mind, pursued by officials and men in protective suits. The minister came on TV. "No cause for concern, none whatsoever," he beamed. The beam was later shown to be radioactive. I continued running until I came to this quiet sunlit valley of tranquillity. The bees hum, the butterflies flit. Here I have built, in conditions of strictest secrecy, my balloon. A balloon! Circular, like God. Or so Trismegistus sayd, bless him. A balloon? A modest affair, not much bigger than a football. Not in the first draft, anyway. Then I got more ambitious. Now it's altogether more impressive, measuring five metres by five, with a volume of eighty cubic metres. In the absence of easily obtainable helium gas I have been eating prodigious quantities of beans and farting into the sack on a daily basis using an old football valve. Now my device is as inflated as it ever will be. Now I am close to the last page. Now the rain abruptly ends, a gust whirls away the dark clouds. The sun, bless its incandescent heart, is coming out! Blue skies – yip! yip! – are here again. Now – swell of an orchestra, boom of a chorus – now I am about to seal my manuscript up in the finest cellophane (please forgive water stains, tea stains, piss stains, pale suspicious splashes, malodorous smears, spelling mistakes, any errors or lapses of good taste). Oozing like the ooze of sadness from J.T.'s mute mouth. In a tight squeeze, he was. Enough of that earthbound throbbing brute. Now I am aiming at the stars. Now I am about to strap my delicate package to the carefully constructed lightweight harness beneath the balloon. A work of genuine craftsmanship, hewn from six supermarket plastic carrier bags. Eyesight dimmer than ever, I see it all. Singing "Faithful Forever" I let go of the string. Wheeeeee! Yaaaaa-whooooo! My dainty craft shoots up into the empyrean, two hundred metres, three hundred metres, a mere speck. If this was a movie "Humidity Built The Snowman" would now blast out. It isn't, it doesn't. At last I found what I wanted, the three posthumous sonatas. I started on the F sharp Minor. Almost gone, now. A dot. Less than a dot. A thermal catches it, whirls it westward! You require assistance. Time to cock your gigantic telescope, you brute! And still my delicate craft grows smaller, smaller. Heading for somewhere nice by the look of it. Enfield Chase! The M25. The Bug River. Potters Bar! How far I know not. Could be anywhere. Bridport. Dores. Shoreham-by-sea. Dunwich. Dragged down by leaks and gravity in the end. I know that tomorrow I shall not pass the Gemmi and get to Thun. I shall not linger at the Hotel Bellevue and then proceed by slow stages down the Rhine to Cologne. Gravity, gravity, it is a grave and heavy matter. My frail craft discovered lying in a grassy meadow where mares graze. Or skulking in *Duck-Lane*, pitifully totter'd and torn. Or wrapped around someone's satellite dish, spoiling the reception. Or falling slap into someone's blazing garden waste, consumed in a trice. Or landing in quicksand, of no interest for a million years until finally, gloriously located by a pretty, cautious, trowel-thrusting linguistically gifted paleopedologist. No, not that, please. No. Saved! Found by you. You, a Barbarian. I have a mind to be very angry. You are a set of people drawn almost to the dregs. You must try another game, this is at an end. *I now walk into the wild. Alex.* No, please! I take it all back. You. One morning. On the way to work. A quick glance. Hmm, this looks interesting. Haven't yomped through a good yarn for yonks. Oh! Heaps of exhaustion! Thinking like Q that the getting to it is taking a long time. Upon a once. Textual/ontological unity well and truly taken to the cleaners. You chuckle and screech, I see it, hear it. Boy, I'd sure like to get my hands on a rope again. Derevaun Seraun! Keep your pecker up. Let's be off to Flint Castle, eh? Good-bye Kansas! Good-bye Wisconsin! Good-bye Utah! Good-bye Uranus! Atishoo! Atishoo! And so on. All good gifts, eh? Taken home later. Cellophane removed and the damp pages given a brisk going-over with the hair drier. You begin, begin, begin. Or fade. A low frustrated mutter. What is all this story about? I was five glass spheres without foliage! Eyes somewhat dimmish grown. Eye am sore eye. Fade sound and vision. Eh, Orrery? Poor Tom. Dr Presto? Madox perhaps. No. No way. It's over. Don't ever leave me, Dolly! No, wait! A late insertion! More good news! The UNICEF annual report has just come out. Last year thirty-seven thousand children under five died every day from malnutrition and easily treatable diseases like measles and diarrhoea, not an easy word to spell. Shit. Is. Hell, I don't like stories with people dying in the end. Said Goldwyn, supposedly. And so that ghostly closing shot, Merle and Olivier's double. Better a riveting climax on a lonely beach, eh? A digitally enhanced pterodactyl's flapped wings. Or some broken-hearted loner walking away down a street while louder gets the last track of *Zooropa*, throbbing as the credits roll. Settled instead for common-as-muck words, the glories of glossolalia. Inspired by *The Replycacion*, a disorderly jumble of skeltonics and eccentric prose, heavy with alliteration, euphistic, *avant la lettre*, accompanied throughout with lengthy marginal glosses. How are you? Fine, fine. To clear away from off the very threshold of despair. All the old. Which we call memory. For information about the Free Presbyterian Church in England and Wales contact BURRYPORT (01554) 833221 or OULTON BROAD (01502) 573641. Eh? Wuzzmoor? Wossmurr in South Asia alone no less than eighty-six million children under five are malnourished! So mustn't grumble, eh? Life here in The Dump not so bad after all. The occasional spurt of melody. Cool blow of a pair of clarinets in the chalumeau register. Art's *Live Across America* album, say. Embedded in treacle, like dinosaur droppings. Or a Fool's Song with accompaniment of strings and harp. And good, very good, to know those foreigners are being kept in their places. Might have a little cerebration later. Ah, the sweet throb of cogitations! With some mastication for afters. A piece of cheese I've been saving. A little carton of flat lemonade. Some Kendal mint cake. Pass the zimmerframe! Forward to the Hillary Step! Must go. Now! Want to see *The Night of the Hunter* again. I've finished here. *In principio erat verbum*. It, this is, truly. All wrapped up. Jacketed in dust. Forlorn. My little capsule of words, sent to drift through space and time, the words growing old and flaky and weird. Talk about the Geystes of Skoggon! How sweet must it be to hang-glide above th'*Aonian* Mount! Klaatu barada nikto! Pipperoo, pippera, pipperum! Hurrah for thermophiles! Adieu bright wit and radiant eyes! Adieu those midnight wranglings over iamb and spondee, anacoluthon and the open vowel. Voice almost gone. *Okay, I won't*. As Ellis said. I mean Elvis. What news? A bit wonky in my left flipper. Invalided out. To this place. The Dump. Invalid. Past my sell-by date. What can I say? With each new draft the number of visitors increased sharply. Such characters! Though demonstrably wrong on such facts as time and place, much of what he recorded has gained currency, albeit no corroboration from any other source. If the cap fits... For the last two decades we've been drifting here in Britain in a thoroughly aimless fashion! *Ubi nunc?* Nowhere. Let's talk. Worms, epitaphs. With rainy eyes. Eh? Be off with you! A skulking, miserable *scholasticus*. Eh? Okay. Thank you for the information. A mere driveller. Become lumber, probably. Cheer up, eh? It is 6.20 pm. We both came to a halt. Ron was muttering imprecations. "Please don't worry too much." I need a change. Bottled oxygen is for wimps. Onward to that abandoned cylinder and survey pole! Though emaciated and indecisive, Alexander is jubilant again. Deaf as the sea, hasty as fire. Eh? Speak up! My brain I'll prove the female to my soul. Since I left you, *I had a most eventful time.* Eh? Naught else but tricks. I feel sore, everywhere. I need a Tyrozet, a splash of after-sun lotion, a kilo of courgettes, a sack of potatoes, a pint of milk. Alas, the *épicier* has cancelled my credit for the last three weeks. The last thing the millennium's crepitant skies require is floccinaucinihilipilification! Ek sal'n plan maak! De secourir ma lâcheté! Et nunc progressi alibi observamus. And Solomon awoke: and, behold, he was hypoxic. It was a dream, yawn. So drowsily I conclude. The doctor made the movements common to a dumbfounder, making the back and elbows move in a series of honesties, dusting his chin with a puff, thinking himself unobserved. All withered, all discoloured. With a smile did then his words repeat. Oh worthless world, oh transitory things! Ah, shaddup, Sol! Shucks. If I could only see the sun just one more time. Brimstony, blue and fiery. Eh? Not true! Stuff univocal order! Double cheers for constructivist epistemology! Don't be so stiff and ill-at-ease. Some have seen (or rather felt) nautical motions and implications. *Mi contra fa diabolus in musica est.* Please, please, plunge and plunge again! Make notes – wheu – - u – - – - u – – – – – – – - if you must. Sit on your rump and scream in Erse! Reinstate the third trumpet! Start, perhaps, by giving up crunching lumps of sugar! What news from Oxford? It's not true what they say about annotation, eh? Plunge into the wastes of all that's used-up, finished with, gone. The distance separating Halifax from Helsingfors has been appreciably diminished. After so many deaths... I think the world's asleep. Flimpf! Resurrect the teachings of Sorbo Soboleff! Or sit quietly. Sit quietly, trap shut. Pretend to be buried in a book. The dew, the rain. As if awake in the midst of sleep. Bah! Boo! Analphabetism? Who? Doctor, Doctor! I think I'm a strawberry! Oh dear. Said the narrator, from whom I wish vigorously to dissociate myself. Eh? A Mardi Gras whim. Was Harlan Potter in on all this? By dint of putting various sixes and sevens together get the whole story bent. Discharged to the last drop and dreg. Eh? A lunatic, lean-witted fool? Not by a long chalk! At last, you think. At long last. The end. Bliss. All together now. In the altogether. At last. Eh? Mar a curious tale. Well, let this pass. One morning... Eh? After all. Eh? When all's said and done. The antic sits. Grinning. Eh? I shall waste no more words, but tell you simply how it all happened. I do not regret this journey, which has shown that Englishmen endure hardships. Oh! A painless piss. Bliss! Eh? Have you noticed that everyone on TV has teeth? Snowed in. Disaster. Yo Ho Ho! I remember there was a clucking of hens from somewhere. Twenty moonshines ago. Once, in a kloof not far from the Letaba... In summertime... All hopes collapse! Now I come to the worst *Pech*. They tolled the one bell only. There is the book, Inspector. I leave it with you, and you cannot doubt that it contains a full explanation of the tragedy. We still don't know why it was done but at least we know *how*. Different worlds remembered and then all put together to form a strange new world. Like perspectives which, rightly gazed upon, show nothing but confusion; eyed awry, distinguish form. Switch them off! Eh? Mais je divague. Parot is my owne dere harte. The train is waiting. Going where? Ah, to Pitchipoi. Crosses, cares and grief. Say hello to Frieda for me, will you? I think I can do better elsewhere. I need at least eleven theses on Feuerbach. Fetch me a Higgs particle! For Pete's sake let's give a party, I feel swell! Take me to Ellis County! I'll see you in the banyuls café at eleven. Deal me a yarborough! The game will soon be up. "Can you keep a secret?" asked Booth. "Yes, yes," said eagerly Robertson. "I can, yes." "So can I," replied Booth. Adwe good nyght. *Crescent in immensum me vivo Psittacus iste.* Give me your hand! Determined still to do our best... I have agreed to go to Zante for a change of air. Fetch me esculents and a bottle of Waters of Moses. Secure me the *mollia temporara fandi*! Dethe dynges one my dore, I dare no lengare byde. Benatewgana! Fut! The sooner we get finished, the sooner we get started. To deal plainly, the fact of the matter is